MW01712594

Rhythm and Blues

Jill Murray

DOUBLEDAY CANADA

Library and Archives Canada Cataloguing in Publication

Murray, Jill, 1977–
Rhythm and blues / Jill Murray.

ISBN 978-0-385-66491-2

I. Title.
PS8626.U775R49 2010 jC813'.6 C2009-904043-3

This book is a work of fiction. Names, characters, places and incidents are products of the author's imagination or are used fictitiously. Any resemblance to actual events or locales or persons, living or dead, is entirely coincidental.

The author wishes to thank the Canada Council for the Arts for their economic support during the writing of this book.

Printed and bound in the USA

Published in Canada by Doubleday Canada,
a division of Random House of Canada Limited

Visit Random House of Canada Limited's website: www.randomhouse.ca

10 9 8 7 6 5 4 3 2 1

One

You know when people say, "It was all worthwhile because I learned so much"?

I hate that.

Whatever doesn't kill me makes me stronger. I wouldn't change a thing. That kind of education is priceless.

Sure, that *sounds* mature, but really, who wouldn't rather get it right in the first place?

I know what I'm talking about. I'm a dancer. Dancing takes practice, but no one ever thinks, *Wow, I'm so grateful it took me eighty-four tries to get the timing right on that turn.* No choreographer will ever chassé up to me and say, "Well, Alya, you've been here three hours, and you still don't know the combo, but I can *feel* that you're *changed,* so we're going to keep you." No one. Not even those touchy-feely lyrical-contemporary types.

"You have to be *honest,*" they'll tell you.

"You have to *pour yourself* into the choreography."

"Those may be *my* steps, but that's *your life story* you're dancing out there," they'll whisper, before wiping away a sweaty little choreographer tear.

You're supposed to be backed by a lifetime of training. It supports you. And in that big moment—the time-stands-still nanosecond when the spotlight finally falls on you—you're even supposed to be a credit to *it.*

But training can betray you, too. I had so much of it behind me, it was all my life amounted to: a training life.

Like I honestly believed that if I practised enough, I'd get to have a real one someday—if I was ever ready to take off the extra wheels or pull out the padding.

When my moment came, my training was useless. Learning is nice and everything, but I want a redo.

I know exactly the day I'd use my time machine to revisit. I can practically see the Reset button. It was last April, a week after my sixteenth birthday.

I'm in this b-girl crew ("breakdance," if you're trapped in the Eighties, but don't feel bad if you are) called the Hydra Force. It's made up of me, Alya (aka Phat Al); my best friend from grade one, Madi (aka Slasher); this hardcore chick from the T-dot, Nadine (Lady Six Sky); and my immature older brother, Devin, who avoids giving out his b-boy name (TypO) because he's afraid someone (our mom) might notice all the walls he's tagged it on around Rivercrest, where we all live (for now, anyway).

In case you haven't guessed already, the Hydra Force is one of the best crews ever to come out of the Greater Toronto Area, or maybe even the entire East Coast, if not the World.

Because of our all-encompassing awesomeness (and practice, and Nadine yelling at us all the time), this other, more established (that means old) crew, Infinite Jest, invited us to practise with them and do shows. Someone has to carry the flame—the almost unbearable flame of undeniable freshness.

That's how I came to be stretching in my best white track pants on the highly suspect floor of an iceless hockey arena, backstage at a festival who-knew-where in Montreal, with Madi pointing out theoretically hot guys and me pretending to care.

"What about *him?*" Madi said, pointing as she reached for her ankle, twisting at the waist so it wouldn't look like she was staring.

"Where?" I pretended not to see. I mean, I *didn't* see. But I could guess. Madi had her types. Indie Fanboy: lanky, unruly hair, puppy-dog eyes, underground band T-shirt. The Digital Camper: medium build, attempted goatee, laptop bag, hiking shoes. Base-Model B-boy: baggy pants, hat over eyes, mp3 phone in use at all times, tattoo in indecipherable script on left forearm. The Post-Reggae Hottie: tall, dark, big easy smile, dreadlocks.

The dude standing at ten o'clock over my left shoulder was a solid P-RH: Madi's favourite type to push on me. I looked up just as he turned our way. He smiled. I thought I recognized him from the sound check. I nodded back.

Madi looked down, giggled, and blushed. "See? Am I right or am I right? He likes you. You should totally get his number," she said, as if I should automatically have been into him because we might be cute together in a matchy-matchy way; as if I was *supposed* to want him because I was a girl and he was a guy. Memo to world: that's not always how it works.

I'd have told her *she* should get his number, but I knew she wouldn't. Madi only ever fell for orange-tanned Abercrombie alpha-jocks—the perma-sneering kind who never returned her calls because they were too busy polishing their own abs.

We both needed to broaden our horizons.

Dreadlocks turned back to the amp he was carrying. I looked back to the floor and deepened into my stretch, partly to avoid Madi's eye, and partly to remind her that my hips were more flexible than hers. She yawned and manoeuvred into a gymnastic contortion I was too dignified to react to, much less attempt. She didn't notice Dreadlocks watching her from across the room.

"*Dix minutes,* Hydra Force! *Scène A.*"

I was startled out of my stretch by the headset-wearing stage manager shouting our ten-minute call—ten minutes for Madi to puke her nerves out three times, ten minutes for Nadine to get herself wound up tight enough to explode, ten minutes for Devin to chatter incessantly, ten minutes for me to stay out of everyone's way and find my happy, focused place.

Backstage was a circus. It had the clowns, the jugglers, and a freak show more entertaining than anything on the three stages that backed into it. Security was practically nonexistent, so every local group had an entourage of twelve friends hanging off them, eating the free food, playing hacky sack, and hitting on people from other acts. A gospel choir was spread out, practising in small groups, trying to harmonize over the speaker distortion spilling from the stage. There were instruments and band gear in every corner, a cluster of DJs who would talk only to each other, and a weird magician's box that was roped off with yellow caution tape. All we were missing were the bears on unicycles and a trapeze artist or two.

On the far side of the tent, Devin recklessly tagged along after Nadine as she paced through her pre-show anger ritual.

"I hope we do a good show," said Madi, starting to fidget beside me as the opening act came off stage. "Do you think we've rehearsed enough? I didn't try my flares once in practice this week. I just hope they like us. Do you think they'll like us?"

"Whatever. Good luck," the exiting lead vocalist said to Madi. "It's wall-to-wall lamewads out there. They're dead. DEAD."

The drummer rolled his eyes. "Don't listen to him. He hates everybody."

But one look at Madi told me that she was already about eight seconds from losing her Larabar lunch to the row of porta-potties to my left.

"C'mon." I grabbed her by the elbow. "Let's walk."

Those last ten minutes before getting on stage are always the worst. Ten minutes is *exactly* the wrong amount of time—generally for anything, but especially for waiting your turn to astound an audience with the brilliance and sheer heat of your dancing fabulousness. Run back to the van to get your lucky bandana and you'll miss your call. Eat and you'll be either indigesting or covered in ketchup by the time you get on stage. Read and . . . nah, forget it. Your head'll be in the wrong place. But just *try* to sit calmly and wait it out, and you'll see: it feels like three hours. The only way to cope is to find your zone. Mine is in my headphones. Bershawn Sera. Whatever his most recent single is. I have adored him since I was thirteen. (Who cares what Nadine says? Music snob.) I want to *be* him when I grow up. (But with breasts, of course.) With Bershawn energy surrounding me, I can only do good things.

I steered Madi to a quieter-ish area not too far from the stage entrance, between a napping yoga priestess and a six-foot-tall cupcake set-piece. I handed her an earbud and began the futile quest to find a setting that would actually allow us to hear Bershawn over all the chaos.

"*Cinq minutes,* Hydra Force," called the SM, the stage manager. Five minutes.

Someone yelped across the room, and I spun around just in time to catch Nadine forcing Devin into a headlock. Madi and I exchanged a worried look, but I was secretly relieved. Tearing the two of them apart (again) would give her something to do. At times like these, it was best to keep her busy.

"Children! Please!" she yelled, running to separate them.

And miraculously, at T-minus-one-and-counting, we were all standing together beside the SM booth at stage right: one unified Force, done battling one another and ready to take the stage.

"Hydra Force *en scène, maintenant, maintenant,* NOW!" the SM yelled, practically chasing us up the short, shaky staircase to the hulking wood-and-pipe-and-lights-and-vinyl-signage stage. Huge but crappy, but huge, it rattled as we walked to our positions. Still, it was a step up from the crowded gyms and filthy clubs we were used to.

The crowd—about three hundred strong—sat on bleachers looking bored. "Give it up *pour Le* Hydra Fooooooorce," bellowed the MC. I liked his style.

The audience clapped politely, and I made up my mind right there to do whatever it took to shake them to their feet. I don't ever want polite. I want ovations and thunder. Preferably, people should weep, but cheering is okay too. No one sits on my shift.

A very long second went by as we waited for the music to start. That moment is pure torture—but in the best way possible. If you play it right, the anticipation makes you stronger.

My knees shook involuntarily as I took my spot. They always do that, no matter how prepared I feel, even if I don't think I'm nervous. To my right, I could feel an almost deadly calm where Madi should have been. As soon as her nerves leave her, it's like everything else does too, and she's able to perform because she's a zombie on stage. To my right, energy radiated off Nadine. On the other side of her, Devin was no doubt fighting to keep his hands still—his nervous habit of clenching and un-clenching amplifies the closer he gets to a stage. But we were there, and we were ready, and we had it under control. So many crews crack up and break up before they ever even get to that point. Not us. We were in it to win it.

At last, the speakers crackled to life and our music kicked in. It was an old-school medley, heavy on the funk—a bunch of James Brown and something called Scorpio and a little Vitamin C and some more of Nadine's favourite old-school breaks. I would have preferred Timbaland or Kanye, but I couldn't fight her on everything. She had the seniority in the b-girl department, and in her eyes, I was probably still just a lowly hip-hopper with light skillz and inferior taste.

I counted to four, waited for the snare hit, and then—*bang!*—exploded into action. I couldn't really gauge the audience response over the music, but I told myself I heard a gasp as we launched into our perfectly synchronized top rock, then dropped down to the floor for a bit of coordinated monkey business. We polished it off with each of us hitting a unique freeze, twisted and upside down, and then we broke apart so we could do our solos.

My biggest challenge at this point was to act enthusiastic and interested for sixty-four counts during which I had nothing to do but clap and react as if I hadn't seen the routine four hundred times already.

Nadine went first—she always has to—then Madi ramped up the crowd's enthusiasm level with a handless flippy cartwheel thing, a throwback to her gymnastics days. I was up next. I jumped out of my spot and ran across the front of the stage, pumping my fist to keep the audience clapping.

I don't have the same big moves that Nadine and Madi do, but I work with the music better. That's why the coolest part of our music was right in the middle of my solo. The music was going through this happy-go-lucky breakbeat bit with lots of brass and cymbals, and I was going all boppy along with it like, *Hi, I'm a cute hip-hop girl like in all the music videos, but with way more talent and slightly less ass-shaking.* And then the sound of a needle scratching the record sliced clear through my routine, and whoa, hey, what? The bass kicked in, so deep that you felt it before you heard it, and then I changed personas, from cute Phat Al to phat Phat Al, and I got all *serious*—not serious like studying for biology, but serious like: *You*—opponent, hater, wannabe—*you* are about to get *schooled.*

Devin went last. He did okay. He gets by on stage because he's funny, and the crowd can never get enough of funny, even if funny is the Funky Chicken. *That* wasn't in his run last time . . . I could already hear the lecture Nadine would yell out in the van later about not changing our act to bring back moves her mother might have done in a velour catsuit at one horrifying time in her life.

We came back together for our grand finale, struck our final pose to the trumpeting close of our music, and . . . the crowd—while not exactly made up of losing-their-ish types of people—they cheered! They stood and they cheered. So much for "lamewads." No one can stay lame for long in the presence of the Hydra Force.

Pumped up by the reaction, we bowed seven times each, and then leaped down the stairs to the backstage tent.

The guys from Infinite were waiting back there to high-five us like always.

"Thanks for warming up the stage for us," said Ender, their de facto leader.

"Watch out—you'll be warming *our* stage someday," said Nadine, laughing and ducking as he moved to knock her hat off her head.

"KID-ding," she said, but I didn't see why it couldn't be true. I'll admit it—sometimes, in between biology exams, I had dreams about making it bigger than Infinite ever had, about taking the Hogtown Throwdown, about getting invited to the Battle of the Year and flown halfway across the world to compete, about shoe sponsorships and TV spots and dancing in movies, the movie they would make *about* us: small suburban crew overcomes lack of cred with surplus of heart. I could see the trailers in my mind. I could see myself in them. I could imagine how smart I'd sound in interviews, and the outfits I'd wear to award shows, and even the airport, and how, if *I* were famous, I'd be one of those celebrities who always look spotless and sound mysterious, and whom everyone loves because they are so gracious to fans and co-stars alike.

It was a super-long shot, and I wasn't crazy enough to actually put eggs in that basket, but was it really so far out to believe we could pick up where Infinite left off and do a little bit better? I didn't think so.

"All right. Enough chit-chat," said Ender. "You guys hit the change rooms. I want you ready to go as soon as our set is done."

"Do we have to?" Madi asked.

"Now!" he answered.

"Sir, yes sir!"

Nadine saluted and ran off, with Madi close behind her. I slowly gathered my stuff and started to follow.

Never mind tour buses and hotels and seeing the world. I'd come to accept that we would never get to see the end of whatever show we were doing, let alone hang out in any of the cities we performed in. No matter how far we travelled, our world would never be any bigger than the inside of the Infinite van, which, I have to say, was a lot smaller than its name would suggest.

But I was not going to rush. Maybe we were nobodies.

Maybe I wasn't even getting paid as much as I would have made staying home and teaching a couple of dance classes at the Movement Spa, my part-time job. But a show well done was its own reward, and I wanted to savour it—at least until my heart rate returned to normal and I stopped sweating, so my track suit wouldn't stick to my back all the way home.

"Al, I mean it—" said Ender. But he got pulled away before he could finish his sentence.

"Yeah, yeah, fine," I said, picking up my bag. I spun around, irritated at being rushed, and—*wham!*—I practically knocked Tall Dreadlocks over with my bag.

"Urgh!" he said, crumpling in the middle. "Whoa, whoa, what's the rush?"

My hand flew to my mouth. "I am so sorry!"

He smiled and bent to pick up the cable I'd made him drop. "I come over here to tell you how hype your show is, and this is the thanks I get?"

I laughed. "Uh, yeah. I mean, usually we like to greet fans with a punch in the face but . . ."

He laughed. "Seriously, you guys were wicked. All the tech guys were losing their minds."

"Thanks," I said.

He craned his neck to look past me, around the tent.

"So, where's your friend? That blonde chick who did the flippy thing?"

"Madi? She's changing."

"Oh. That move was *insane.*"

"Yup. She's pretty strong," I said.

And then Dreadlocks said nothing. The conversation had taken a turn for the awkward.

"Uhm . . ." he finally said. "Tell her congratulations for me?"

A slow grin spread across my face. He was totally into her. Not me. *Her.* This was good. He was—what?—maybe eighteen? Just older enough. And friendly. Cute. Responsible enough to hold down a real job. He gave off a good vibe.

"Here," I said, taking out a pen and scribbling Madi's number on the back of the show flyer. "Congratulate her yourself."

I could worry later about whether she'd kill me when she found out.

Dreadlocks smiled, a little confused, like maybe he wasn't used to strange girls handing out their friends' numbers with no provocation. Then he looked at the number again.

"This is long distance?" His smile faded a little.

"Not *that* long." I waved it off, feeling just a little sorry for him. "We're here pretty often."

"Thanks," he finally said. "I'm Trevor, by the way."

"Al. Later?"

"I'll see what I can do."

And there was that smile again: broad, warm, friendly, somewhat shy-ish. Any feelings of potential remorse I was developing evaporated. There was something *right* about this guy. Just not right for me. As he walked away, I mentally patted myself on the back for a good deed well done.

Then, Madi came out of the tent.

"Hey, why aren't you—?" She trailed off as she noticed Trevor walking away, slipping the flyer into his pocket. "You gave him your number?" she squealed. "You did, right? Do I have a good eye or what? Omigod. Alya gave out her number to a guy. On her own. An actual living, breathing guy!"

I smiled. "His name is Trevor," I told her, and I ducked into the change room.

Two

I changed as fast as I could, knowing it still wouldn't be fast enough for Infinite. Sure enough, everyone was gone by the time I was ready. I slung my heavy duffle bag over my shoulder and raced an obstacle course around performers and gear, trying not to get tangled in the flapping wings of choir robes as I dodged and wove my way to the exit.

I stepped outside, expecting empty parking lot as far as the eye could see. Instead, I was shocked to find several rows of screaming children and parents squished up against the temporary metal barriers leading out of the artists' area.

The rest of the Force was trapped by the crowd, reaching for the pens and programs kids were holding out to them.

"What *is* this?" I yelled to Madi over the screaming.

Madi shrugged, like, *I know! Crazy, right?*

There were normally a few people waiting for Infinite at the end of our sets—mainly b-boys who hung back and pretended they just wanted to bump fists before easing into the matter of some event they wanted to invite them to. Sometimes there'd be a kid or two and a couple of self-appointed Defenders of the Old School. They'd shrug and mumble and blush until they got their autographs, and then retreat as quickly as possible. Sometimes someone got hold of Ender's ear and refused to let go, and then he'd have to invent a way out.

Meanwhile, we would stand at a safe distance and smile and watch and be ignored. It was Infinite that had the history, Infinite that had the fans. We were a cute way to give people a bigger show, but people were not *interested* in us.

But something had changed.

"What do they *want?*" I asked Nadine.

"Your autograph, genius," she said, handing me a pen.

"It's her!" one of the little kids up front yelled, and suddenly the crowd shifted to surround me. The barriers barely held up against their weight.

"Oh. My. God."

The others were so much farther along the line, they made it out before I was even halfway through.

"Hurry it up, Al," Ender warned me before making his break across the parking lot, flanked by Madi and the rest of the crew.

"Catch you at the car," said Devin, following them with Nadine, waving to the kids as they left.

"No!" I yelled after them. "Do not leave me here by myself!"

I was surrounded by begging faces. They were shoving pens at me and asking questions and telling me I was awesome. I couldn't just *leave.*

"Where did you learn to do that?" a little girl asked me.

"From my crew and from Infinite."

"Have you been on TV?" asked a boy.

"Not yet, but wait . . ."

"What's your website address?" said a mom.

Crap. I *knew* we should have been thinking about getting one. "Look for us on VideYou," I covered.

I didn't mean to stay *that* long, but by the time I was done, the sun was starting to set. I said goodbye to the last kid—this little dude with red hair and rollerskate shoes—and I picked up my bag for what I hoped was the last time.

And that's when a long shadow fell across my path.

"Hey," said a voice at the end of the shadow.

I looked sharply to my left. Standing there, leaning against the barricade, was a man dressed like every Hollywood tabloid skeez in recent memory all stapled together.

He wore gigantic white Adidas, as bright as Madi's mom's teeth. They had the huge tongue and the fat laces undone, so they were practically licking the sidewalk. From there, standard men's tube socks slouched over his ankles, and brushing the top of those was a pair of . . . I don't know what you'd call them, exactly. Shorts? Capris? Let's say baggy grey manpris, at least two sizes too large. Then he had on three shirts with popped collars, the top layer of which was Lacoste. His mesh track jacket hung open so you could just see the logo. His pockets bulged with lumpy objects, and around his neck were tangled several chains, a small mp3 player, a phone, and gigantic headphones—which were ironically not plugged into anything. A thin strip of hair crept down from behind his ears and ran around his jaw, as if to indicate where a beard could have grown if he'd wanted one. His head was covered in greasy stubble and topped with a plaid fedora, tipped to one side.

Omigod, get his number! the miniature Madi I carry around in my head squealed. He was the exact, perfect example of every single way I am *not* into dudes.

"Hydra Force, right?" he said, smiling and holding out his right hand as he walked towards me with an arrhythmic limp I guessed was meant to be a gangsta lean.

"Yeah . . ." I said, taking an unconscious step backward.

"You were terrific out there."

"Thanks." I wished Madi had stuck beside me. She could have created a disturbance. We could have escaped.

Alone, there was no way I could squeeze past this guy. He was blocking my path out of the artists' corral, which now seemed more like a trap than a tunnel to safety.

"No, I mean, *you,*" he continued. "The *group* is fine, but you—*you* were fantastic."

I looked at him like, *okaaaay.* Because that was a lie—an outright lie. As far as b-girling goes, the crew *is* fantastic. But me? I am pretty and trained and I do my job. That's it. Nadine is the soul. Madi is a force of nature. Dev and I are just hard-working and lucky. If you want fantastic from me, ask for hip hop or jazz and I'll make you shiver with fantastic. But suggesting that I am fantastic at b-girling is like saying that Nadine is nice, or that Madi is totally chill, or that Dev should lighten up a little. I mean—*get real.* I adjusted my bag, gave Styleguy my best *I-wasn't-born-yesterday* look, and prepared to make a break for the van.

"I don't want to hold you up," he said, following me into the parking lot, "but there's this group I'm putting together. Your look would be perfect for it."

"My *look?"* I said.

"Yeah," he said. "Have you ever done any modelling?"

"No," I answered emphatically, picking up the pace as I upgraded Styleguy to Potential Molester.

"You're so fresh and original," he said. "And EnChantay—they're going to be huge. These girls are headed for the Grammys."

"Oh, sorry," I said, relieved to be off the hook. "I don't sing. I'm a dancer. And I already have a crew."

"Dancer?" he said. "Singer? Those are just labels. My job is to find *real* talent. I've got a sixth sense. And I could see it from a mile away: you're the real deal. I don't want to diss your friends—you're all very cute together and it's obvious you've got the break thing down solid—but you're the real *performer* of the group. You have *it*."

"*It?*" I repeated, not even trying to disguise my disdain.

"Everyone wants it, but no one knows what it is," he said. "Star quality. *It*."

I winced.

He took a step back. "I probably look like I'm trying to pick you up or something, right?" He reached into his pocket and handed me a business card.

Terrific. If he kidnapped me, now I would know just what to call him (Réjean "RJ" Cormier—Producer) and where he wanted me to think he worked (Soul292 Records, 292 Avenue de la Morasse, Montreal).

"You know what that is?" he said. "That's a division of Capitulation Music."

I wanted to throw the card out, but a flash of recognition surged through me. Capitulation Music was *Bershawn's* record label. For just the tiniest microsecond I felt curious—I almost wished it could actually be real, instead of the scam it definitely had to be. I frowned harder and set my mind against even thinking about it.

"Just try out," said RJ. "That's all I'm asking. If it's not your thing, you can say no later. Hell, *we* can say no later." He laughed to himself like that was the funniest joke in the world—like no one ever said no to RJ Cormier.

"I don't even live here," I said, edging farther away. "I'm from Toronto."

He shrugged. "No problem," he said. "I'll be there next week. We can set up an audition."

I craned my neck to squint at the van. I could see Madi, shielding her eyes against the setting sun, looking for me.

"How old are you?" RJ asked me suddenly.

"Sixteen," I answered automatically.

"Hot." He snapped his fingers and pointed at nothing in particular. "I love it."

"Okay, gotta go!" I practically yelled.

"Our website's on the card," he called after me as I ran to the van. "Look us up. Call if you want to find out more. Don't let your talent go to waaaas—"

The end of his sentence was cut off by the sound of the van door sliding shut.

"Omigod, drive!" I said as I squeezed into the second-to-last row, beside Madi.

Ender glared at me in the rear-view mirror.

"What do you think you were doing out there? I realize your fans need you, Miss Phatty Phat Phat, but my son is going to starve, naked and homeless, if I don't get us all home in time to make my shift at the hospital. You know *work,* right? It's that thing my kind of people have to do to keep your kind of people alive until you're legal. When is that again, anyway?" He checked his watch. "How soon can I start driving off without you when you make me late?"

"Two more years," I said, sticking my tongue out at him. "What do you care, anyway? You're, like, *famous.* You shouldn't need a job."

He laughed so hard he almost rolled the van into a ditch.

"Al, honey, baby, let me explain something important to you. B-boying is like doing almost anything else worthwhile: you practically need a second job just to afford it in the first place. We're not famous like your whatshisname—*Bershawn*—is famous. We're barely more famous than *you* are famous. You cannot eat fame or feed it to your kids, so if you're in this vehicle for any reason besides keeping b-boying alive, your life is going to be very disappointing."

I frowned.

"Duh," said Nadine, but she pulled her arms in around her, and I knew she felt the chill too.

"It's not like I was *trying* to be late," I said, as if making the conversation more annoying would somehow make it less depressing. "Aren't you guys supposed to have my back? That guy out there was creepola. I could be in the trunk of his car right now, and you wouldn't have noticed."

"You're here now, so don't complain," said Ender. "He can't have been scarier than that chick who showed up to every single battle in 2007, asking Mephisto to sign her breasts."

Mephisto woke up briefly in the front. "Oh, man . . . I can't believe I forgot about her."

"You want to be famous, Al?" Ender droned on. "You gotta put up with the people who make you that way."

"He was, like, *your* age, and he thought it was *hot* that I was sixteen," I said.

The back half of the van went "*Ew.*" Nadine made a puking sound.

Ender laughed. "Wow. Who actually says that out loud?"

"RJ Cormier," I told him, reading from the card.

"Cormier. Why does that name sound familiar?" Ender drummed his thumbs against the steering wheel. "Can I see the card?"

I fished the already crumpled card out of my pocket and passed it forward. He looked it over without taking his eyes off the road.

"Soul292. Right! This guy was a producer on that shoot we did last year for that video for that chick—the one where we had to do backflips all day. I couldn't walk for a month after that. But, Al, this guy is legit. He's the real deal."

"He's creepy."

"I don't think he meant *hot* like you think he meant hot."

"What other way is there?" I whined, almost offended.

"The way that means you're not a thirty-six-year-old b-boy with back problems. Like you're young and unspoiled and you have your whole life ahead of you. The record industry loves that. They feed off it. Too young is just right for Capitulation Music."

"How is that not creepy?"

"Al, this guy may be cheese, but he is what he says he is. You want to spend your life on stage, 'not working'? RJ Cormier is exactly the type who can make that happen."

I pictured RJ again in my mind's eye, all done up in his oversize clothes, like a gigantic toddler. I still had my doubts.

"I can't believe this!" said Madi, leaning back in her seat. "I leave you for five minutes and you get signed to a major record label. Typical."

"I'm not signed to anything. This whole thing is just weird. I can't even sing," I said. The last thing I needed was her getting jealous over something I didn't even want to do.

Mephisto chimed in, "I don't want to insult any of your little pop gods or anything, Phatski, but as far as I can tell, that hasn't mattered in a long time. You should try out."

"Yeah," said Devin from the back seat. "Let them notice on their own how much you suck."

There was an audible thud, and then a squeak, as Nadine sucker-punched him in the ribs.

"We all know that if you audition you'll get it, so you might as well drop this fake modesty crap," said Nadine.

"That's not true!" I said. "Besides, why would I audition? I'm with the Hydra Force. We'll be famous *together* someday."

"That's sweet," said Mephisto. "But if that's what you really want, you should be doing anything you can to get the most exposure you can, *right now.* Once everyone knows you, you can do pretty much anything you want with the rest of your life, and bring whoever you want with you."

"I can't believe you're being so negative about this," said Nadine. "If it were me I'd ditch you in a second."

I took the business card back from Ender and sat back in my seat, trying to make sense of the whole thing. If I were to get the gig—not that I was even sure I wanted it yet—I would have had to rethink everything I'd been planning for so long. This was how my life was scheduled to go: university in a couple years, probably studying biology, or maybe exercise science or something. That way I could have it both ways—dancing *and* something to fall back on later. I liked the Plan. My parents liked the Plan. Even my guidance counsellor liked the Plan.

But none of those people had even half the experience that Infinite did on stage. What if Ender was right and the Plan wasn't enough? What if, to make it, you needed an extra push from somewhere, or a bigass heap of luck? Creepy RJ didn't exactly seem like the fairy-godmother type, but what if he knew something I didn't? What if that was my bigass heap of luck waiting for me out there in the shadowy parking lot?

"You know you have to call him," Madi said. I knew she was probably right.

Three

I blinked and yawned my way off the train and into school on Monday morning, gripping my contraband coffee for strength. (I wasn't allowed coffee at home, but there was a stand at the train station. I'm, like, five-foot-nine. What did I care if it stunted my growth?) Going back to stone and ivy and uniform blazers after a weekend of dancing and loudness and b-boy stink was always a shock. Like, *Was I really there? Am I really here? What is all this?*

I waved hi to a girl from my biology class I didn't know that well. Even though it was a small school, a lot of us never got a chance to hang out because we were all so *busy* most of the time.

My school, Rosewood Academy for Girls, was set up to "promote achievement." Don't be fooled by the flowery name. It was no "finishing school," except in the sense that everyone seemed to be constantly racing full out for some distant, invisible finishing line. The halls were thick with junior national fencing champions, patent-holding science nerds, one eight-year-old ninth-grader, and half a dozen of those girls you see in CBC documentaries who coordinate computer initiatives for Third World high-schoolers. I don't know what they were thinking when they decided to give me a scholarship. Compared to most of the girls there, I was a total lightweight. So I taught a couple of dance classes. So what? No one's going to cure cancer with Elementary Jazz.

I originally applied to Rosewood only because Madi wanted to go, having hated her first year at Rivercrest High. We'd been joined at the hip since the day she showed up at my public school in grade one. Her family had just moved to town, and instead of bringing her inside and making sure she found her class, her parents had just dumped her at the door before driving off.

I'd spotted her then, standing alone in the middle of the playground, chalk-pale, looking panicked (although she would never admit that). Her blond ponytail was tied up in the prettiest blue bow, and I raced Matthew Wilson across the sandpit to be the first to say hi to her.

"I'm Alya. What's your name?" I said.

"Mad-i-son." She enunciated every syllable.

"Are you lost?"

"No." She forced a shrug. "I'm just waiting."

"Want to go on the slide?" said Matthew.

"If you come with me, you can share my Froot Loops at recess," I said.

"Okay." She nodded.

I grabbed her by the hand and dragged her to meet everyone I knew. That was at least half an hour before we figured out we were next-door neighbours, and by then we were already good friends.

I didn't hold my breath waiting for a big green Rosewood acceptance envelope to arrive in the mail: I never believed I was in the same academic league as Madi. I assumed all along I'd have to put up with four years of Rivercrest High School without her.

When the envelope did come, I was shocked.

"Congratulations, Miss Merchant. In recognition of your high verbal aptitude, exemplary science scores, and demonstrated potential in the performing arts, Rosewood Academy extends a warm invitation to join our community of future leaders."

I had to read the letter five times. I'd thought I was just a bun-head. Turned out, I was a *verbose, nerdy* bun-head, and there were people out there willing to risk the reputation of their institution on just how much *more* verbose, nerdy, and bun-headed I could become.

Madi got in too. We were so excited. We were going to private school! We would wear matching uniforms and take the train. We were going to be the coolest girls on campus. (We really believed that.) We threw ourselves a party for two, with a cake-mix cake and party hats left over from a birthday a million years ago.

But that was as far as the whole plan got. I didn't get a scholarship offer, and without financial aid, it was RHS or bust for me. And Madi's parents flat out refused to pay for her. Her mom doesn't think twice about spending $800 on a pair of shoes, but private school? Forget it. If public school was good enough for her, it's good enough for Madi.

"Well, at least we still get to go to high school together," said Madi.

"That uniform is probably scratchy anyway," I pointed out.

"And we still get to be the coolest girls in school!"

Do I even need to say that it didn't happen that way?

My first week at RHS was a disaster. The school was ridiculously big, and I was taller than everyone in my grade. Then there was "the black thing," as one of my teachers decided to put it, like it was some craaaaazy show I was putting on just to get noticed. I didn't even know where to start with that one. Only in Rivercrest could you actually get away with thinking something like that, let alone saying it. I looked forward to a time and place when I could leave it behind.

As if I didn't already have enough problems, a day or two in, this gross guy started hitting on me really rudely four times a day, and his girlfriend—because somehow he had one—started a rumour and got half of my class mad at me. Even the friends I had hung out with every day in grade eight started to treat me funny, and soon, just walking through the halls was a nightmare. *I'm not even into guys, especially not that one!* I wanted to yell, only, of course, not really, because letting a little piece of information like that out was the last thing I needed. In a place like Rivercrest, it's best to be as normal as possible, and I could already tell I was *not*.

I was pretty sure I would have to admit I was different someday. But I wanted to keep someday far away as long as possible. Life seemed complicated enough already.

Keeping someday at bay, straining to play normal while dodging evil notes, glares, and spitballs, I could barely pay attention in class. My teachers thought I was a slacker, and when I had an audition that Friday, they refused to let me out for the afternoon.

All of that happened in just *four days*. To hear Nadine tell it now, that's a pretty average week at RHS, but my mom wasn't having it. She spent half the week on the phone, arguing with my principal. Then, out of the blue, she got a voicemail message at work on Thursday:

"We're so sorry about the late timing, Mrs. Merchant, but there has been an opening on our waiting list, and Rosewood Academy is now able to offer Alya a scholarship. Would she still be interested in attending?"

My mom ditched work in the middle of the morning and drove straight to RHS to yank me out of there. She considered pulling Devin, too, but he would have been distracting in a Rosewood skirt.

Madi was disappointed.

"I don't *have* to go," I told her to be nice, even though I knew I did. Rosewood would mean a fresh start and a new identity.

"I'd hate myself if you stayed just to keep me company," she said. "Go. You're gonna kick ass. I can handle these people."

She was the best friend anyone could ever ask for, and I was going to have to spend the next four years without her.

All Monday morning, RJ's business card burned a hole through my shirt pocket, and all morning, I made up excuses why I couldn't call him. Before homeroom, it was too early. Everyone knows music people don't get up before noon. Then I was in class, and . . . well, that's *class*. You'd better be on fire if you even think of using your phone in class. At morning break, I didn't want to seem too eager. Then, oops, class again.

It's one thing to know you need to do something and another thing entirely to take out your phone and dial the number of a creepy guy you met in a dark parking lot, even if he does work for a major label.

The half of me that wasn't freaked out was convinced that when I called, RJ would be all, *Alya who?* and deny we had ever met. Or I'd get to the audition, and then he'd hear me sing and say, *I know you said you* didn't *sing, but you didn't tell me you* couldn't *sing. That was just . . .* And then he'd start puking into his Red Bull.

I mean, sure, I sang in the shower, walking to the train station in the morning, in the change room at dance class, while I did the dishes, on study breaks, at b-girl practice—but only 'cause it felt good, not because I thought I knew what I was doing. The last thing I wanted was to be like some piece of reality TV roadkill who thinks she rocked the audition when actually she completely sucked, and then she gets pissed at the judges because she can *feel* in her *heart* how good she is. Real singers work at it. Hard. They sing like I dance. I only dance like I dance.

I tried not to obsess over it, but that's like someone telling you not to think about rhinoceroses, or to ignore your breathing. *Great, now I can't think about anything else.*

Ender's dire warnings about poverty and fame did windmills around my brain all morning. In between them, I thought about all the places a music career could take me—and how I might even get to get out of the van once in a while if I went there without Infinite—about convincing RJ to put the Force in EnChantay's music videos, about the amazing outfits designers might give me to wear to award shows.

Okay, that was all a little much to expect. I hadn't even auditioned yet. I was *afraid* to audition. But when I'd thought big before it had always worked out—that was how I'd got myself into Rosewood—and some of my best dance auditions were the ones that scared me the most, like when I had to convince Nadine to let me into Hydra Force.

In the end, it was fear itself that made me do it. So what if I was bad? What if I could actually trick them into taking me? The idea was so ridiculous, I practically *had* to try out.

At lunch, I finally accepted the inevitable, took out my phone, and called Réjean (RJ) Cormier, producer at Soul292

Records. The phone rang only twice. I was expecting an automated greeting, and then a receptionist to deal with, but RJ himself answered right away.

"Yo," he said. No *Hi,* or *RJ speaking.* Just *Yo.* It took me a second to put my words together.

"Hello?" he said, impatiently.

"Um, hi," I said, remembering my own phone manners. "This is Alya Merchant. We met yesterday at—"

"Ah-haaaaaah," he said. "Phat Al herself. You called!"

"Yeah . . ."

"Hot. I knew you'd make the right choice."

"Thanks?" I said, not sure that I wanted RJ approving my choices.

"Are you calling why I think you're calling? You ready to set up an audition?"

"Yeah, I—"

"What are you doing this afternoon?"

I stammered. "*This* after—?"

"Yeah, like, three-thirty? Can you get out of school? You are in school, right?"

"Yeah . . ." I said, momentarily distracted by the idea of RJ standing up for education.

"Hot," he said. "Love it. Bring your best song."

"Uh . . . okayyy—" I said. I'd worry about skipping my afternoon classes after I'd already done it.

"You have a way of getting here, or you need me to send a car?"

Oh, right. Like that sounded safe. "No, I'll—"

"Great, then."

He rattled off an address and a buzzer code, and before I could process what I'd just agreed to, he hung up.

What had I done? *Three-thirty? Best song?* I didn't even

have *a* song, let alone a best one. No time for panic. I shoved it down, pulled out my phone again, and called the one person who could help.

Devin groaned when I asked him to drive me. "I was going to actually study for once, Al. But what are *you* about to tell me I'm doing?"

"I'm not *telling* you anything. But I kind of have this audition all of a sudden with that RJ guy from Montreal. Can you come get me? Like, now? I *need* your help."

"No!" he said, but I knew he'd come through. He always did.

"You're the best, Devin. I'll meet you at the back door at two."

It wasn't until I hung up and was putting my phone back in my purse that I looked down and realized *all I had to wear was my school uniform.* I redialled in a panic, but Devin wouldn't pick up.

I hightailed it to the bathroom for emergency wardrobe triage. The situation was this:

- Hair pulled back tightly into bun—we had to wear it this way at all times or cut it short.
- Starchy-stiff white shirt, buttoned all the way to the neck. Hot, meaning stifling.
- Scratchy-stiff hunter green double-breasted blazer, worn at all times while in class. Hotter.
- Hunter green and brown-burgundy plaid pleated skirt, worn exactly to the kneecap, no exceptions, enforced with regular ruler checks. Willy-nilly skirt rolling was not going to fly at Rosewood.
- Thick, and I mean *thick,* green knee-high socks, worn to exactly half an inch below the kneecap

(with mandatory replacement at the first, slightest hint of slouching).

- Hunter green tie, Windsor knotted, just in case the outfit wasn't already green enough.
- Truly horrible heavy black oxfords with chunky soles and—shriek—*Velcro* instead of laces. It was a miracle no one had mutinied.

This was no Britney-Spears-sexy-bad-girl-circa-1999 school uniform. This was serious, regulation stuff. And it was itchy. I can't believe I once looked forward to wearing it. I looked like a child. I looked like a man. I was not going to be able to turn this around by unbuttoning a button or getting creative with the tie. The nice people at Soul292 were going to take one look at me and think I was trying to sell them a chocolate bar to support the scholarship fund.

In a fit of desperation, I remembered my gym uniform, clean and folded on the top shelf of my locker. I ran to get it, and back in the bathroom, I pushed the heavy grey jogging pants down low on my hips. Then I knotted the T-shirt at the waist to give it some style, green though it was, and tugged it so it dropped off one shoulder, revealing a glimpse of my oh-so-stylish sports bra. I had my black running shoes with the gold stripe, so my feet were taken care of. I pulled all the pins out of my hair, shook out my braids, then piled them back up on my head and used my tie to coax them into a high, wild ponytail with bits of awesome poking out in every direction.

I took a step back from the mirror and checked myself out. I still looked more like a janitor than a future star. Thankfully, my makeup bag was stocked. I went heavy on the eyeliner and the bronzing powder, and finished it off with dramatic lips—but not so dramatic that I couldn't go outside without feeling like it was Hallowe'en. I checked myself out again. Much better. If I tipped my head to the side and squinted so everything went a little bit fuzzy, I could almost picture myself as an extra walking by in the background of a music video.

The rest I would have to make up for in posture and attitude—two areas I usually own.

Devin was obviously excited about the big fancypants label audition, but he had to act annoyed in the car anyway.

"Nice outfit. They gonna make you run laps?"

"Ha ha. Are you finished?"

"No. I was going to say, remember the time you went to that audition, and you had underwear stuck to the leg of your pants?"

"Devin! Please!"

He laughed. "Or that other time when you had braces, and you tried to bite that thread off your sleeve, and it got caught and you had to go in with your wrist glued to your face?"

"Devin! Come on. I have, like, an hour, and I don't even have a song yet!"

"Sure you do. Just sing that Bershawn one that sounds better than the other ones."

"I have a Bershawn song that sounds better than the others?"

"Yeah. You know the one. *Baby, baby . . . baby, something . . .*"

I hummed a few bars. "Is it that one?"

"No. The other one."

Okay, honestly? Nadine is right about one thing: *most* Bershawn songs go *Baby, baby, something* . . . Fortunately, there were only, like, ten or eleven of them I sang on a regular basis, and only five that I'd let Dev hear, so after a few minutes of humming, we were able to figure out that it was "(You) Mean the World (To Me)" that he was talking about.

"Really? I would have thought 'So-So Special.'"

"No. That one's okay, but your voice does this cool warbly thing on the *No-o-oone* part in the other one."

"I have a warbly thing?"

"Yeah. Just make sure your underwear's on the *inside* of your pants and you're gonna be fine."

I smacked him in the arm.

"Hey!" he yelled. "Driving!"

Traffic was heavy, but we pulled into the parking lot of Capitulation Music at three-thirty on the dot. Cap Music occupied a big, old converted warehouse in Liberty Village, just on the edge of Nadine's old 'hood in Parkdale. I recognized the area from the Hogtown Throwdown, which was always just a few blocks over. There were eighteen-foot posters of Cap artists running along one wall of the building, including, of course, Bershawn. My heart started to beat a little quicker. I closed my eyes, did some serious breathing, and gripped the door handle tighter to try to control my nerves. *I am a professional, I am a professional, I am a professional,* I told myself. When I opened my eyes, I almost believed it.

"All right, ready?" said Devin.

"As ready as I'm gonna be," I said.

"Let's go," he said. "Audition's not going to happen in the car."

"You're coming in with me?"

"Hell, yeah. This RJ dude might be the real deal, but that doesn't mean I trust him alone with my sister."

As we walked across the Cap parking lot, I high-fived the bottom of Bershawn's poster for luck.

Four

Inside, the Capitulation Music HQ was all concrete and brick and exposed beams, like they forgot to finish it and then decided they liked it that way. A short receptionist with lopsided hair simultaneously answered three calls, accepted a package from a courier, and waved us down a hall after making us sign a guestbook. We followed the signs to Studio 12, which was in the basement at the bottom of a long staircase, the walls of which were decorated with magazine covers. (There were two Bershawns: May 2005 and February 2009.)

I held my head high and put on my big, happy audition smile as I pulled open the heavy glass door and made my entrance into the studio lobby, expecting RJ to be waiting for me. But inside was just another receptionist behind a heavy black desk. This woman was a lot calmer, much taller, and very blond. Her hair was pulled back into an intimidatingly sharp ponytail, under a wire headset. She didn't look up from the notes she was taking as I stepped up to the desk.

I must have stood there, not sure whether she was actually on the phone or not, for five minutes, and in that time, I looked around the room, slowly losing my cool. There was a whole different vibe down in the basement. The walls had been finished with a kind of rough stone material, and all the furniture was done up in chrome and black lacquer. There was brown-beige carpeting on the floor and a couple of leather couches around a glass coffee table topped with a collection of serious-looking music production magazines, a candy dish, and a bowl of guitar picks. Framed gold and platinum records ran along one wall. The couches had electronic control panels and headphones built into the armrests. A small waterfall ran in one corner, its babbling highlighting the otherwise extreme quiet that stifled the room. This place was *luxe.*

Devin threw himself down on one of the couches and put on a set of headphones. I made a small throat-clearing sound, and the statue receptionist finally looked at me.

"Do you have an appointment?"

"Yes, I'm Alya Merchant, here to see RJ Cormier?" I felt about five years old and three feet tall in my grubby gym uniform and showgirl makeup.

She sighed and walked wordlessly down a narrow hallway that led off behind the waterfall.

Unsure what to do with myself, I sat down on a couch opposite Devin. He motioned for me to rub lipstick off my teeth, then laughed at me when I did.

"Psych!" He laughed. "Relax, Al, it's going to be fine." He tossed a guitar pick at me. I caught it and put it back in the bowl.

The world's most talkative receptionist came back and gave us a wary look.

"Mr. Cormier will be with you shortly."

"Thanks," I said.

She winced, like, *Ew, it spoke to me.* Devin stifled a laugh behind his hand, then looked at his watch and yawned. I picked up a magazine, but I was too nervous to read it. I thumbed through the pages and looked at the pictures while going over Bershawn's lyrics in my head. I knew the song. I could do this. Really.

It was different from a dance audition. There was only

me, instead of me and thirty girls in Lycra nervously pacing up and down the halls—no catty, over-competitive psychos to give me the evil eye, but no familiar faces to kill time with, gossiping about the choreographers, either.

After ten minutes, RJ finally appeared. I heard him coming before I saw him, his gigantic RJ pant legs brushing against each other as he swaggered down the hall.

"Phat Aaaaaaal!" he said, and I jumped up from the couch, a little too eager.

Today he was wearing head-to-toe denim, from his hat right down to his shoes. His jacket was the same shade as his pants, and even his shirt had a vaguely acid-washed texture. Behind me, Devin broke into a coughing fit. RJ snapped his fingers and asked the receptionist to get him a glass of water, but I knew it was laughter he was choking back.

"RJ, wassup," I said, recovering my cool, like I hung out at record labels every day, no problem.

"What am I *not* up to?" he said. "This group is gonna be *sick,* straight up, no joke."

I wondered if he always talked like that, or if he was putting it on just for me. Something told me he was always putting it on, period.

"People are excited about this, Alya," he continued. "I got guys in New York calling me, setting up deals. Everyone wants to know: *RJ, when we gonna see an EnChantay single? When's it gonna drop?* I'm telling you, EnChantay is gonna change the game."

I nodded to cover for the fact that I didn't really know what he was talking about. What guys? What deals? What game?

"RJ, this is my brother, Devin," I said. Dev removed the headphones.

"Make yourself at home," said RJ. "Have you eaten? Do you need anything? Inga, call the man a pizza, will you?" he yelled to the receptionist before Devin could say no. "So, Al, Alya. Can I call you Al? Are you ready? Let's do this."

"I'm always ready," I said.

He snapped. "Love it."

He led me down the hall and around the corner into the studio. There was a huge desk loaded up with expensive-looking recording equipment. It smelled expensive, too—all plasticky, woody, and carpety new. Facing the table was a wide window into the next room, which was smaller and empty, except for some microphones and music stands. It was as spotless as if it had never been used before. There wasn't so much as a speck of dust on anything.

RJ squeezed out some hand sanitizer from a dispenser on the wall before sitting down at the console.

"So what have you got for me?" he asked, leaning back in his chair.

"Oh, um . . . '(You) Mean the World (To Me)'?" I said, drawing the brackets with my fingers in the air before realizing I was doing it.

"'Mean the World'? Why'd you pick that? A *dude* sings that."

My body temperature dropped another twelve degrees. What was he getting at? Would he reject me automatically if he thought . . . ?

"Uh . . . I . . . uh . . ." I sputtered. "I really respect Bershawn Sera as an artist," I finished quickly. If there was one place it was more important to act normal than Rivercrest, it was at auditions.

He grinned. "Ah, don't worry, don't worry. I'm just playing with you. Let's see your music." He held out his hand, and then I choked with panic again. Did he want me to sing along with the CD? I could have brought it in with me, I guess, but that would have been really weird. I mean, I like karaoke as much as anyone, but seriously—

"Sheet music . . . ?" he said, hopefully. "So we can accompany you."

"I don't have that," I mumbled to my feet.

"That's okay, our keyboardist can probably figure it out. What key you gonna sing it in?"

"Key?"

"Ohhh-kayy," he said. "Change of plans."

I winced apologetically.

"Inga," he said, leaning into an intercom. "Tell Matty to stay upstairs. We're not going to need him after all."

He pulled a cover over the keyboard in the corner and turned back to me.

"Just for you, Al, I'll make an exception, just this once. You can do it a cappella."

He led me into the next room.

"You ever been in a vocal booth before? Ever used a mic?"

"No." I shook my head, pretty sure at this point that karaoke wasn't going to count.

"Okay, it's real simple," he said, gesturing to the mic, which was large and silver and had one of those mesh things in front of it, like in all the videos for Bershawn ballads. "Don't stand too close, don't bump into the spit guard, and don't turn your head while you're singing, or the sound won't go in the mic and I won't hear you. Cool?"

I nodded.

Before leaving the room, he handed me a pair of oversize headphones like Nadine is always wearing (which I respect her for, but I would never try in public, for fear of the impact it would have on my outfit). I put them on, stepped up to the mic, and waited for something to happen.

Suddenly RJ's voice was inside my head. "Anytime you want to start, honey, you just go ahead," he said into a mic on his side of the window. I jumped.

Oh. Me. *I* was supposed to happen.

"Um, okay," I said into the mic. The sound of my own voice in my head startled me. I sounded so . . . dry. Loud. Ugly. Not at *all* smooth and warm and sexy, like real singers on the radio. If I thought the microphone was going to magically transform me into a Grammy-nominated recording artist, I was obviously crazy. But, luckily, I didn't think that. RJ did. RJ was *crazy.*

It was a little late to worry about that. Stuck in the booth with him staring at me, I had to do *something.* I took a breath, leaned into the mic—and froze when I realized I had no idea where to start.

Crazy RJ drummed his fingers against the table on the other side of the window. The longer I didn't start singing, the worse it felt, so I closed my eyes and tried to imagine, as hard as I could, that I was just in Devin's car and the intro to the song was coming on over the stereo. I imagined Bershawn talking out the intro over the low, rumbling bass.

Oh baby, baby, baby, bayby, bayby, baaaybeh
C'mon
Yeah now
Try it, you might like it
Everything gonna be all right

I counted out the remaining beats, snapping quietly with my hand at my side. I let myself sway in time, heard the music swell in my mind, and when I opened my eyes, by some miracle I sang.

Girl, there's so much I wanna know about you
That no else has ever asked, I bet
U are the one, that much I know to be true

I was so self-conscious. My voice was shaky and nervous. I knew I was too quiet, even though I was trying not to listen to myself.

I must have looked like a total freak, swaying back and forth to an imaginary beat, staring into the mic like I was going to make out with it, but what else could I do? I had to get myself into the song somehow. I could feel the fun part coming, and I leaned into the chorus with every little bit of feeling I could dig out.

Be-cause baby, baby, baby, bayby, bayby, baaaybeh
No one understands but you
No one understands for sho-o-oh
This bond we got
Can't be broken
A bond of understandingness

Did my voice do the warbly thing? I couldn't tell. But the momentum from the chorus swelled in my chest and pushed me into the next verse, and for just a second, I could almost feel something click. My voice in the headphones came out strong then, smooth. The end of the song was so close now—

"Okay, that's enough!" RJ barked into the headphones. The lights came on in my mental club. *That's it, pack it in, get out,* said the bouncer.

"Oh, um, okay . . ." I said, starting to take off the headphones.

"No, no, don't go anywhere," said RJ, smiling. "We've got one more thing we need you to do, and then you can go home to your boyfriend or your homework or whatever, a'right?"

I cringed.

"This is what we're going to do," he said. "On this CD is a rough mix of the very first EnChantay single. *No one* has heard this. This is special, and *you* are lucky, because I am going to play it for you."

"Okay, thanks!" I said, thinking that sounded too easy.

"The *second* time I play it," he said, "I want you to harmonize with Angelique and Julie, the girls on the tape."

"How do you want me to do it?" I asked, trying to sound intelligent.

"Any way you want. I need to hear what kind of ear you've got. Improvise. Make it sound hot."

"Okay, let's do it . . ." I said, my voice shrinking in my throat again. It was one thing to sing a Bershawn song I'd had memorized for years, but *making up notes* over *professional singers?* It took everything I had not to rip the headphones off my ears and run out of the booth, but I kept it together.

A high-pitched sound beeped in the headphones four times, and then a beat kicked in. I nodded my head in time, thinking that was the cool, into-it thing to do. Then the vocals kicked in. One high Beyoncé-style voice *whoa-o-o*-ed and *yeah-ah-aaa*-ed all over the track, while a second, thinner voice sang out every other word in a plain, rhythmic, almost toneless style.

Why-u-gotta-be-up-in-mah-grill-when-u-know-I-take-care-a-mah-self?

This was not going to be easy. How was I going to get a word in edgewise? Where was there room in this song between the *yeaaahs* and the sing-talking and the three frenetic lines of bass and drums and high-pitched electronic blips that criss-crossed each other in mid-air like a laser fight? A girl could lose an eye trying to make harmony in that mix.

"A'right, you ready?" RJ asked, licking his lips as he cued the song back to the beginning.

"Sure," I squeaked.

"*Whyyyyy you go-o-ta,*" I sang, picking a way lower note to start on than Angelique or Julie, and stretching it out so it just kind of hung under the rest of the line in the song. "*I-take-care-a-mah-self,*" I sang, jumping back in at the original pace. I didn't totally pick the right notes right off the bat. I could hear in my head what I *wanted* to do, but my throat sang something kind of different. *Not good, Al. Not good.* I tried to nudge it into the right place the second time the chorus came round, but I don't know if I hit it or not. RJ's face wasn't giving anything away. It looked like he was texting on his phone the whole time.

"Okay," he said, yawning, as I finished. "That's all we need to hear. You can go. Thanks for coming by."

"Thanks—" I started to say, but by the time I got my headphones off, he was already out of his seat and walking away. What had just happened? Did I do okay? Did I suck? I already knew I'd sucked. I wandered out of the studio and back to the waiting area in a disoriented stupor, the stress of the audition quickly replacing itself with post-suckitude depression. I had skipped lunch and risked a detention for *that?* What was I thinking?

"So how'd you do?" Dev asked as we stumbled out into the parking lot.

"Don't ask," I said, dragging my feet to the car.

Thank god I'd never have to do *that* again, I thought as I sank into the sagging passenger seat.

Five

Devin dropped me at home and then peeled off to who knows where in his rusty car. My parents were out at a convention and wouldn't be back until late, which was just as well because I wasn't in the mood to talk to anyone. I wanted to lock myself in my room with a plate of last night's leftovers and my math homework, and discreetly and exponentially function myself into a polynomial trance until I forgot the EnChantay audition had ever happened.

I had just dug into my third problem and fourth mouthful of eggplant bharta when the phone rang.

Madi. "Hey, what's going on?" she asked.

"Not much," I lied. If I'd mentioned the audition, she would have started to panic about what would happen if I got the gig and had to leave the Force, then she'd have called Nadine and arranged an emergency crew meeting so we could hold hands and plan for the future. No thanks. The sooner I stopped thinking about it, the sooner the whole Alya-tries-to-sing fiasco would be over.

Lucky for me, there was something more pressing on Madi's mind.

"So, um, I don't know how to tell you this," she said, "but I got this really weird call last night."

"Ooh!" I said.

"I'm *really* sorry I didn't tell you right away," she said, sighing, "but, like, I just wasn't sure how you'd take it, you know? I didn't know *how* to tell you."

Sometimes Madi can be really dramatic. Some little thing hits her a certain way, and by the time she tells you about it, she's convinced herself the world is about to cave in. Still, I couldn't imagine who could have called to make her feel guilty for twenty-four hours.

"Tell me what?" I encouraged. "Are you kicking me out of the crew?" I laughed at my own joke.

Madi drew in a big breath. "We're friends no matter what, right?"

"Oh god, you *are* kicking me out of the crew!"

"Alya, I'm serious."

"I can hear that. *What* are you serious *about?*"

"Okay," she said. "I guess there's really no other way to tell you—"

A hundred more seconds went by—enough time to finish carrying the six and adding. (I was trying to train myself to be fast without a calculator.)

"Trevorcalledme," she finally said, so fast I could hardly pick the words apart.

"I'm sorry, what?" I put my pencil down.

"See?" she said. "See? I *knew* you'd be mad. That's why I didn't tell you yesterday."

"Whoa, whoa, whoa. Madi, I'm not mad at you. I don't even know what you said. Try again. Slower this time."

"Tre-vor caaaaalled meeeee," she said, drawing out each syllable.

"Who?"

There was a long silence on the end of the phone—a silence that told me I was missing something, a silence that sent my mind racing through the disorganized file system of my brain, the one that looks a lot like the desktop of my Mac: a billion little bits of information, some related, some not, all piled in towering stacks according to the last moment each one seemed important—dance steps piled on biology facts, on Hydra Force drama, on a whole bunch of RJ and the EnChantay audition, my laundry, Nadine's parents calling to check her alibi. Within the first three layers at least, I could find no mention of anyone named Trevor.

"Trevor from Montreal!" Madi nearly yelled. "Cute Trevor! Dreadlocks Trevor! TREVOR YOU GAVE YOUR NUMBER TO!"

Oh, snap! *That* Trevor! Oh. This was bad. How was I going to sound not mad, but not so not mad that she'd figure out that I gave him her number instead of mine? Then again, how had she not figured that out already?

"You don't *remember?*" she said. "Alya, if I didn't know you so well, I'd be thinking you are completely slutty right now."

"I dunno," I said. "Things at school have been really crazy lately. I've been distracted."

"Alya, have you *ever* given out your number before?"

"Yeah! I have!"

No, I hadn't. I let other people do it for me.

"I just . . . just thought . . ." she stammered. "I mean, he seemed so . . . Oh, I don't know. I just thought that this guy was the one."

I laughed. "*What* one?"

"Well, okay, not *the* one the one, but you know, like it might actually work out. Like you two could hang out next time we were in Montreal, and you'd actually like him for once, and then you'd talk on the phone and send e-mails and stuff, and it wouldn't even matter that it was long distance because then it would be really special when you got to see each other, and it would be so cute and—"

"Madi, you're worse than my mom."

My mother would never admit it, but she gloats when her friends complain about their daughters' boyfriends, and unlike Nadine's mom, she's never even suggested I try dating the dorky sons of people she works with.

"What was it?" Madi prattled on. "Was it his breath? I thought his breath would be okay. He looked like his breath would be okay."

"You want me to pinpoint what made him not interesting enough to remember?"

She let out an exasperated laugh. "I just don't understand why there is a problem with *everyone*."

Neither did I. Not entirely. I mean, I could see, objectively, that a guy, like this Trevor dude, was hot and would be cool to hang out with, but once I was alone with him, it always seemed to end with him feeling more like a brother—a much less annoying kind of brother than my actual brother, maybe, but still not someone I wanted to make out with.

"So Trevor called me, not you, and you don't remember, so it's not even news," Madi recapped, deflated.

No!" I said. "It *is* news. Trevor called you! Yay! What did he say?"

"I don't know. He's not even my type, really."

"Why not? Didn't his breath sound as good as it looked?"

"No, it's just he's—"

"It's because he's black, isn't it?" I said.

"I was *going* to say he lives out of town," she retorted.

"Again, you wanted *me* to go out with him. You thought it would be 'cute' and 'special.'"

"And we have different goals," she rattled on. "He's not in school or anything."

"That doesn't mean he's not smart. It doesn't even mean he won't ever go to school. It just means he's confident enough to do what he loves."

"See? Trevor really would be better for you."

"Except that he's *interested* in *you.*"

She was completely silent on the end of the line.

"Where did he get my number, anyway?" she said suddenly.

"Uh . . . probably the show phone list?" I said, covering as best I could. "Maybe he's friends with the stage manager."

"What is he? Some kind of stalker?"

"Nooo . . ." I said, speaking slowly and thinking fast. "I think it's very . . . resourceful. And nice that he'd make the effort."

"I think it's weird."

"That Todd guy actually *did* stalk you, and you went out with him for three months."

"That was different."

"Like I said, it's *the black thing,* right?"

She sighed. "You know how it is in my family."

"Who cares what it's like in your family?" I said sharply. "Even when you do exactly what they want, they're never happy—"

"Okay," she said. "But won't he eventually figure out that I'm a dork?"

My irritation melted. I rested my forehead against my desk.

"Talk to him. If it doesn't work, you have an easy out because he's from out of town."

"You're right," she finally said, laughing at herself. "I'm probably making way too big a deal out of this."

"Definitely," I said.

"What are you doing right now?" she asked. "Do you want to come over and study?"

"I can't. I really, seriously have to work tonight," I lied, because I knew I wouldn't be able to look her in the eyes and not say anything about the audition. "We goof off too much when we study together." We may be nerds, but we're only human.

"All right, then," said Madi. "See you at practice."

"Yeah. Catch you later."

I hung up and went back to my homework. I told myself I didn't even want the gig. But every time I came close to losing myself in a problem, my mind would boomerang back to the audition. I would hear myself reaching for a note and missing, and see the strain on RJ's face. Too bad I couldn't ditch myself for the rest of the night.

Six

Three weeks later, I was asleep on my face when my phone rang. It was a PA day Friday, so I was at home. The morning before, I'd been up at 5:00 a.m. to cram for a test. Then I'd done a whole day of school, taught not one, not two, but *three* dance classes—my own usual Baby Jazz, plus assisting with the adult beginner jazz and ballet—then had a Hydra Force practice, sort of, and watched a movie, mostly.

My parents were at work, Devin had class, and before my phone started blasting Bershawn's "Never Dance Again," I had been getting a good start on catching up on a week of sleep in one day.

I rolled over, picked up the phone, and, in my half-awake state, hit Answer instead of Reject. Damn.

"Hellooo?" I groaned painfully towards the receiver, fumbling to bring the thing to my face.

"Alya, that you?" an only distantly familiar voice shouted.

"Yeah?" I mumbled, rubbing my eyes. What time was it? Not quite noon. This was not okay.

"Ha haaa . . ." said the voice. "Was someone *asleep* in the middle of the day?"

"Yeah," I said. "Who *is* this?" But I don't think he heard me.

"Ha haaa . . . just kidding, just kidding. I love it. You're still hot. Don't worry."

Oh.

"Hi, RJ," I said.

Hang on. RJ? What? my brain screamed a half second later. What did this mean, this RJ being on the phone? I propped myself up on one elbow.

"Long time no speak!" he said, laughing. "But I've got news for you. Great news!"

"Oh?" I said, skeptical.

"I shopped your demo to my backers, and you know what they said? They said, *RJ? How do you do it? Who is this kid? How soon can you get her?* You know what that means, Phat Al?"

"No?"

"It means, Miss Alya, that you, Alya Merchant, are the newest member of EnChantay!"

Stunned silence was the best reaction I could muster. I had not considered the possibility that I would actually get the gig. It was illogical, irrational, *impossible*—the kind of thing that could only happen while I was half-asleep—*dreaming,* in other words. "You are the newest member of EnChantay!" was a sentence that belonged to the same alternate world as flying pigs and cheesemares.

"So," said RJ on the other end of the phone, "is that hot? Do you love it? Whaddya say?"

"Wow," I said, visions of tour buses starting to circle slowly around my head. "Are you sure?"

He laughed.

"Am I sure? Alya, I am always sure. I am the king of sure. Of course—"

Aha, I thought to myself. Here comes the "but," the "psych!" the man jumping out from behind the bushes, *Candid Camera*–style, laughing.

He continued, "Of course, we should probably have you come to Montreal, just to see how you fit in with the other girls before we make anything final. Can you do that?"

"I can't miss any school," I said reflexively. Exams were coming up, and I needed to ace math and all my sciences to get in to my honours classes for grade twelve.

"That's cool, that's cool. I respect that," he said. "What about the May 2-4 long weekend? Could you come up for that?"

"Uh . . ." I couldn't think of any reason not to. If I planned carefully, I could still get all my studying in.

"Do you need to talk to your parents?" he said. "I've got a train ticket with your name on it."

"No!" I said, almost violently. I still hadn't told them anything about the audition. Devin hadn't said anything either. He might be a joker, but that is one pact he never breaks. We *do not* tell our parents things about each other. Not without checking first. Not without signing documents.

Madi and Nadine would totally kick my ass if they ever heard me complaining about it, but my parents, Wallace and Jean Merchant, are the most supportive people on Earth. That sounds good on the surface, until you realize that support has a stifling, anaconda-like, hug-you-till-you-die quality to it.

Unlike Nadine's parents—vultures who circle, waiting for her to fail so they can swoop down and hand out demerit points—or Madi's—who basically laid her under a rock seventeen years ago and then flew off to Switzerland, promising to come back when she was perfect—mine don't have rules as much as they do "benchmarks for success." (That's my dad's favourite phrase. He owns and develops franchise restaurants, so he talks like that pretty much all of the time.)

If I mess up, I don't get grounded. I get pulled into a "strategy meeting" to discuss the implications of my behaviour. Grounding doesn't sound half bad to me. It would be so *quiet*. I'd have so much personal space. I could, I dunno, go up to my room and *do my homework* without having to think up a polite way to excuse myself from a power dinner. *Sorry to eat and dash like this—I know this face time is vital—but in order to meet the science-aptitude benchmark required for the implementation of Phase Three of my Evolving Life Plan, I really must devote at least one point five hours to Biology of the Human Being before 9:00 p.m.*

Bra shopping, how my friends are doing, fights I have with Devin about sharing the TV in the basement—I don't always want help with my "challenges." Seriously, is life ever that challenging? *Wallace, I'm cancelling my three o'clock. Alya has a hangnail. Should she bite it off or use clippers? We'll have an answer by dinner.*

"No," I said to RJ. "It's all clear. They're cool. I can make it. I'll be there."

"You're a star, Alya!" He yelled, louder still, "This is gonna be huuuge!" Then he hung up, leaving me almost as confused . . . okay, *more* confused than when the phone had first rung.

I flopped back against my pillow, but sleep was so over. How on Earth was I going to sneak off to Montreal?

Twenty minutes later, I was sitting at Madi's desk, pretending to memorize fun facts about Canadian history and mentally running through my conversation with RJ on high speed, over and over again. She was lying with her head at the foot of her bed, feet in the air, halfheartedly revising her English essay.

I cleared my throat.

"So, hey, remember that RJ guy I met in the parking lot in Montreal at that Infinite show?"

"Omigod," said Madi, always eager to beat me to the point. "You got an audition?"

"Yeah . . ." I said, cautiously.

"That's awesome! When is it?"

"A couple of weeks ago."

She sat up and stared at me, not understanding.

"I kind of . . . got it already," I continued. "Maybe."

Madi gasped. "You didn't say anything!"

"It just went, like, *really* badly. I didn't want anyone to know," I said.

"Not even me? It can't have been *that* bad. You got the freaking job!"

"Well, not exactly. RJ still wants me to go to Montreal to see how I 'fit in' before he'll make it official."

"You'll fit in," she said dismissively.

"You don't know that."

"Alya, you'll fit in because you always fit in," she snapped. "God, you're so annoying sometimes. It's like everything comes so easily to you that you don't even notice it's happening."

"I—" I started, but honestly had no idea how to finish. "I'm sorry I didn't tell you."

"It's fine," she said, in a voice that told me it wasn't.

"I said I'm sorry."

"I said it's fine. When do you go, anyway? What did your dad say?"

I hesitated.

"Omigod," she said. "You didn't tell them?"

"No," I admitted. "Would you have?"

"But you can't just go to Montreal alone. What if RJ *is* a creep after all?"

"Are you lecturing me?"

She rolled her eyes and flopped onto her back so her head was dangling off the foot of the bed.

"How are things going with Trevor?" I asked her.

"Are you trying to change the subject?"

"No. Yes. Tell me anyway. You know you want to. It's *Treeevor,*" I sang out.

"He wants to come visit," she said.

A not-entirely-selfless plan began to form in the back of my mind.

"Or," I said, "you could visit him . . ."

"I don't know," she said. "I don't want to lead him on."

"By going on *one* date? Madi, everyone risks leading everyone on on first dates. It's what they're *for.* By your logic, I've done nothing *but* lead people on. What if it's fate? I have my audition *in Montreal.* You need to see Trevor *from Montreal.* Coincidence?"

"Yes," she said.

"No, it's a sign—a sign that we are meant to take a secret road trip together."

"Which is supposed to work *how?*"

"You tell your parents we're visiting my cousin in Montreal, and I'll tell *my* parents we're visiting *your* cousin in Montreal." Suddenly it all seemed so easy.

"My licence doesn't even let me drive on the highway," she said.

"We'll go on the train together. I'll tell RJ I can only come if you come with me."

Her brow furrowed, but a tiny smile started to tug at

the corners of her lips. “My parents *cannot* find out about Trevor,” she said.

I grinned. “Isn’t that half the fun?”

“I’ll think about it,” she said.

“To Montreal!” I said, raising my water glass.

“Not so loud!” she said, raising hers.

“It’s official!” I whisper-shouted. We were definitely going.

Seven

Next thing I knew, I was sitting opposite Madi in "Elegance Class," on a train bound for Montreal, thanks to some upgrade coupons her mom had. The car was only half full, so we were able to take over a whole four-seater like we owned the place—me with my biology homework, Madi with a stack of books spread out all around her. (We were such rebels. No wonder our parents bought the cousin story.) A woman passed periodically with a drink cart, supplying us with endless refills of coffee. Out the window, the sun glinted off Lake Ontario like the glare off RJ Cormier's fake bling. I relaxed back into my seat, content to put off doing my homework and imagine we were on a girls' weekend.

"Are you nervous?" asked Madi, putting down her homework and picking up the *Sizzle* magazine I had bought at the station.

"Hell, yes," I said. "Thanks for reminding me."

"You're going to be famous," she said, almost resentfully.

"Whatever. Even if they decide to keep me, which they probably won't, I just want to make the most of the experience and learn whatever I can. That's it."

"Yeah, right. Listen to yourself. You're already talking like an *Idol* contestant."

"Hand me that *Sizzle,*" I said, to change the topic.

"They're going to love you," she said. "Even if you don't get famous from this, you will someday, so they might as well just give it to you and get it over with."

"Ahem," I said, grabbing the magazine and flipping straight to the quiz to change the topic. "Question number one: 'You're moving in for a kiss with the guy you like when suddenly you notice it: nose hair! Do you:

A) Turn your head and puke into your purse—you got it on sale anyway?
B) Close your eyes and remember how nice his hands are, and how good his car smells?
C) Braid it—it's not a problem if it's not in the way?'"

"That's disgusting," said Madi, stifling a laugh.

"Answer," I said.

"Okay. C."

"Next question: 'You're at the beach when you spot a guy with a smokin' hot bod. You let him know by:

A) Rubbing your eyes and blinking at his six-pack abs.
B) Rubbing your shirt against his washboard abs—while you're still wearing it.
C) Rubbing a brick of cheese against his razor-sharp abs—it's almost lunch and you are *hun-gry.*'"

"That's it," she said. "I'm having a nap."

I smiled. Target disabled.

When we got to Montreal, we got off the train and hauled our bags up to the cab stand—easier said than done in my case. My bag was almost bigger than I was, and twice as heavy. Having no idea what I'd be expected to do or wear all weekend, I had packed for every possibility—casual, dressy, sweaty, pretty, whether or not the hotel had a swimming pool, if we were going to go out, if it rained, if it was unseasonably warm. I had old comfy pyjamas, funky sleepover pyjamas, bags to go with everything, extra running shoes, makeup, hair stuff, my own pillow (because, like Oprah, I need my beauty rest), and the stuffed sheep I'd slept with every night since I was six.

"I'll give you this much, Al," said Madi, as she helped me drag the thing from the taxi up the stairs of the bed and breakfast. "You're already packing like a diva."

As it turned out, we were staying at a bed and breakfast in a big stone townhouse opposite a park. Our room was huge, with two big, comfy beds, wood trim everywhere, and best of all, a claw-foot tub in the bathroom.

"This, I could get used to," I said as I took it all in.

Madi took her shoes off and tentatively climbed up on one of the beds.

"Ooh, bouncy," she said, starting to jump. "Okay, I'm going to call Trevor."

While Madi was on the phone, I availed myself of the excellent water pressure and had an excessively long shower. Then we went out to dinner, returning early enough to watch half a movie, stuff ourselves with chocolate, and still get enough sleep to be wide awake at eight o'clock the next morning. In retrospect, for two girls out on a weekend pass with no parental supervision, we were almost wastefully responsible.

"Pressing question," I said to Madi as I tried to put together an outfit for the next morning. "What should I wear tomorrow?"

"Skinny jeans, my gold tank under your black meshy sweater thing, and boots. You did pack my gold tank, right?"

"Um. Yeah. Sorry?"

"Al, this is bigger than sorry. Wear the tank."

"It's not too much?"

"For me it would be, but on you it's perfect. Why'd you think I let you keep it so long?"

Shortly before midnight, I crawled into bed and turned out my light, but I couldn't turn off my brain. It had been easy not to think too much with Madi distracting me all day, but now, my thoughts were loud enough to keep me awake. How would I know if I was "fitting in"? Would the other girls know the songs already? Would they expect me to? What if I couldn't learn fast enough?

The next morning I went to the closet, took one look at the outfit I'd put together the night before, and scrapped the whole thing. I didn't have the confidence for fussy pants or gold anything. Instead, I defaulted to the security blanket of outfits: my comfiest jeans, a soft T-shirt, a warm hoodie, and my Pumas.

"You're going like *that?*" Madi said when she came out of the bathroom.

"I don't want to look like I'm trying too hard," I said.

She narrowed her eyes at me. "It's your freaking record deal. If you're not going to look like you're trying *now,* when are you?"

"Okay," I said, and grabbed a black ball hat and some sunglasses. "There. I'm ready."

We went downstairs to the breakfast room, where I couldn't sit still and everything tasted like wood. Even the croissants caught in the back of my throat. We got two coffees and hailed a cab.

"What are you going to do after you drop me off?" I asked Madi as we started to move.

"I'm going to come inside long enough to make sure these people aren't 'psycho killers,'" she said, like she was my mom or something.

"You don't have to do that," I said uncomfortably. "Aren't you meeting Trevor?"

"I am, for lunch," she said. "I have time. Why? Are you embarrassed? I can't say hello? You're just using me for an alibi now?"

"No—"

The cab jerked to a stop and the driver shouted something indecipherable at us over his shoulder. I looked out the window. We were pulled over at a nondescript intersection with a rundown convenience store on one corner, a dull, grey warehouse building on the other, and a couple of old, dusty brasseries rounding out the other two.

"What's going on?" I asked. "Where are we?"

The driver shouted again.

"I think he's saying we're here," said Madi.

"Where?"

"Here. At the studio."

I looked out again, confused. There was no one out on the street.

"Really? The studio in Toronto was so—I mean, it was like something out of a music video. Everything was . . . shiny. Are you sure?"

"Have a great day!" Madi said, and then she settled back into her seat like she was waiting for me to get out.

"Aren't you coming with me?"

"Nah. You don't need me."

I gripped the door handle and swallowed my pride. "Madi, I think I may have spoken too soon. Please, will you come into the studio with me until we are sure these people are not, as you say, psycho killers?"

She smiled. "I would be delighted, Alya. Thank you for asking."

We got out, and the cab peeled away after a dramatic U-turn. Walking around the building, we found a grimy glass door—the only one marked with a number. I had to bump it with my hip to get it to open. Behind it was a narrow staircase with peeling paint and a faint gasoline smell.

"You're *sure* this is the right place?" Madi asked as we climbed.

"292 Avenue de la Morasse, the one and only," I said, trying to keep a positive outlook. Maybe they wanted to keep a low profile so they wouldn't be mobbed by fans.

We were greeted on the second-floor landing by a heavy, black steel door with a tiny, fresh, but already peeling Soul292 sticker just above eye level. I relaxed a little as I pulled it open and saw that, inside, the studio was basic, but kind of calm and comfortable-looking, with a glazed grey cement floor, a piano, and some stereo equipment on an area rug off to one side, and a full wall of windows letting in the soft grey light from outside.

"Hello?" I called into the empty space. I walked over to the windows and looked out over more grey stuff: a bridge, criss-crossing train tracks, old factory buildings, in the distance a narrow canal.

Madi plinked at a couple of piano keys, and the notes floated out into the room like an unanswered question: "Hello?"

"Maybe I should call RJ," I said, walking into the far corner of the room. But before I could dial, something freaky happened.

"Hey!" barked a voice right behind me—not Madi's. I caught my breath and spun around. There was an angry-looking woman sitting at a folding table behind the support pillar. She was dark, lean, and muscular, with broad shoulders and long hands, no makeup, and ironed-straight hair pulled back in a tight, low ponytail. She looked like a tennis pro.

"Do you mind keeping it down? I'm on a deadline here," she said.

There were loose papers spread out all over the table—lyrics or something. She was frantically writing or rewriting something on a fresh page.

"I'm so sorry. I didn't see you. I'm Alya." I offered my hand, but she didn't shake it.

"Réjean will be here shortly," she said and turned back to her writing.

I stuck my hand in my pocket and tried to casually make my way back across the room to where Madi was standing, hugging herself nervously.

"Who is that?" she mouthed at me.

"I don't know!" I whispered back.

Suddenly the main door crashed open, and RJ Cormier stormed through it, passionately yelling into his phone in mile-a-minute French. He was wearing a suit—black turtle-neck under black collared shirt under black jacket, with black leather tie, black pants, black running shoes, and . . . a black pirate bandana. The tail of it swished as he whipped his head around in reaction to his conversation.

I looked over at Madi to gauge her reaction, but she was studiously maintaining her no-reaction smile.

"Okay, bye!" RJ said, abruptly ending his call and turning to us with open arms.

"Phat Aaaaal, how's it goin'?"

"Great," I said weakly. "RJ, this is my frie—"

"Madi! AKA Slasher! I remember from your show!" he yelled, taking her hand in both of his and shaking it vigorously.

"Julie!" he yelled across the room. "Come over here. I want you to meet someone!"

"We met," the woman, whose name I gathered was Julie, yelled from behind the pillar. *Right,* I realized. *Julie. From the tape.* I guess she sounded . . . *nicer* when she was singing.

"Deadlines," RJ explained with a wave of his hand. "Julie's our magician in the songwriting department. Eagle eye. Spots problems from a mile away, fixes them."

"I can hear you, RJ," Julie yelled across the room. "Maybe if you didn't hire shit songwriters, I wouldn't have to—"

"So," RJ yelled into my ear, throwing an arm around my shoulders, "what do you think of the space?"

"It's . . . *different* from the Cap studios in Toronto," I said.

"Ha haaaaaaaaa," he laughed. "Yeah, this far from the mother ship, we gotta top the charts on a budget. It's how it always is when you're starting out. But someone's gotta do it! Charts ain't gonna top themselves, right? After you hit number one, they'll give you the keys to your Beamer and gold-plated bathroom."

Madi nodded skeptically.

"Don't worry," said RJ. "The renovations are almost done, and then it'll really be something. We've got everything we need here. Lots of space, and it's not ready yet, but we're building a recording studio back in there." He pointed to a door behind Julie's pillar. "And an office for me. Need to keep that casting couch somewhere, right?" he said, elbowing me. "Ha haaaa."

Madi glared at him.

"I kid, I kid," he said. "There's barely room in there for a desk. We're strictly profess—"

He was interrupted mid-sentence by a knock.

"Aha!" he said. "The missing piece of the EnChant*ing* puzzle."

He stepped dramatically to the door and swung it open.

Madi and I both gaped. The girl on the other side was maybe two or three years older than me and tiny, but Amazon somehow as well. Maybe it was the four-inch heels on her alligator boots. Maybe it was the jeans, so skinny they could have been pressure-moulded. Or maybe it was her jacket—short, feathery, disappearing at the collar into her hair, which was intimidating in its sheer volume.

She stood framed by the doorway, striking a helpless yet dominating pose, with a two-foot-tall latte in one hand and a hockey-sized shoulder bag dangling precariously from the other.

"Angelique!" said RJ, letting the door fall shut behind her and hurrying to air-kiss her good morning. "Only forty-five minutes late! To what do we owe this record?"

This must be the lead singer, I thought to myself. There was just something about her—a magnetic quality that made it impossible to look away. Even standing still, she made you wonder what she was going to do next. I shrank as I stared.

She handed RJ her coffee, dropped her bag, and walked right through me to where Julie was sitting. Julie got up for her. They hugged. Angelique whispered something.

Julie whispered something back. They laughed. Angelique abruptly turned and walked back towards me.

"What's this about?" she said to RJ, lifting her chin in my general direction.

RJ threw his head back and laughed. "Angelique Fielleux, may I present to you Alya Merchant."

"She brought her babysitter?" she said, pointing to Madi with one very long acrylic nail.

"No, actually, I'm just on my way out," said Madi. "But nice to meet you."

Good thing that wasn't embarrassing, I thought to myself, covering my face with my hand.

Madi turned awkwardly towards me. "Later," she said. Then she moved to hug me, but stopped herself and instead bailed directly into the stairwell with a self-conscious wave.

"All right," said RJ, rubbing his hands together as the door clicked shut and Madi's footsteps faded down the stairs. "Let's get started!"

Eight

I found out that morning that I had been breathing wrong my entire life. Sixteen years: in, out, in, out, and I thought things had been going pretty well—I was alive, seldom passed out, and could even take six or seven flights of stairs at a jog without running out of breath. But the first thing my new vocal coach told me—after sighing and rolling her eyes—was, "Are you even aware that you *have* a diaphragm? *Calisse,* we're going to have to start from scratch."

Yes, my vocal coach was Julie. Apparently she was responsible for practically everything EnChantay did. Perhaps that's why she didn't have time to dress better or moisturize, I thought uncharitably, my frustration getting the better of me.

"Just my luck," she said. "Like I don't have enough work already. I swear, these people—they pick some random, clueless . . ."

I stood straight and took it. Her criticism was nothing compared to what I had endured in Mrs. Grimp's ballet classes, and I wasn't six anymore, so she couldn't scare me.

"At least you have good posture," Julie finally said. "The last two girls—"

My eyes bulged a little. Last two? What had happened to them? Were they buried behind the drywall in RJ's new office?

"They didn't work out," said Julie. "Every time RJ tells us he's found 'the total package' he brings me another teenybopper with a nice ass. If you could sing out your butt—"

"How long have you been with EnChantay?" I interrupted, desperate to say something to take the heat off me.

"Since before there was an EnChantay," she said. "RJ brought me over from another group he was trying to make that didn't work out as well. I keep telling him it should be a duet, but he's hung up on this idea that we need three girls."

This was what it looked like when a group worked *well?*

"As long as we have to be here," said Julie, "let's make the best of it. Now, our lungs don't just puff out, they expand *down* into our stomachs, and that's the way we want to breathe when we sing: into our ribs and stomach. So forget everything you know about flat abs, and let me see you breathe. Let your gut stick out every time."

I realized she'd probably delivered this speech a million times before, just as I had a few Baby Jazz lessons I could teach half-asleep.

I tentatively let go of my stomach, which, I admit, I'd been holding in as tightly as possible for about a decade, ever since Mrs. Grimp had poked my belly and made me tell the class why I wanted to go through life looking like "that bear from the root beer commercial." It took a few tries, but with Julie glaring at me, I finally breathed as deeply as I could, until I felt my stomach stretch so much it hurt. My nervousness worked against me, gripping the air tightly, clutching it against my chest.

"You're a nose-breather," said Julie. "You're going to need to get over that. We need our air for singing. We don't have time to wait for it to travel all the way through our nasal passages. In through the mouth. Out through the mouth." She paused. "You don't smoke, do you?"

"No."

"Good. 'Cause you'd have to give that up, too."

I didn't know if I was allowed to stop breathing yet, so I kept doing it: in, out, in, out, through my mouth into my belly. It didn't quite help me relax, but I did start to feel light-headed.

"Unclench your jaw," said Julie. "Let it hang open. Don't be afraid to look silly."

Easier said than done. I felt like any moment I was going to forget English and start drooling. After half an hour of breathing, I was starting to worry that we would never get to the part where sound comes out.

"All right, you're ready for humming," Julie said suddenly.

I couldn't hold back my disappointment.

"You don't want to hear how I sing before we go through all of this?"

She stared at me for a good ten seconds.

"No. Why? You want to end up like Cammie?"

"Who's that?"

"You, three girls ago."

"No, I—"

"Then no more questions."

I hummed, with my jaw still relaxed ("Relaxed, relaxed, relaxed!" yelled Julie), and let the sound make my lips buzz together in a way that reminded me of the time Devin dared me to lick a nine-volt battery. Once my humming was deemed satisfactory, I was allowed to move up to saying the letter A over and over again, drawing it out, trying to press the sound out with that muscle under my lungs.

"Control it," said Julie. "Don't let air escape all around the note, and *don't* tack an H onto it, whatever you do."

"Am I doing anything right?" I started to ask. But just then, RJ swung the door open.

"Union break, girls!"

Julie was out of there so fast she almost knocked him over.

"How's it going, kiddo?" he asked me, his jacket still blowing in the breeze of her roadrunner-like exit.

"Good?" I answered, automatically.

"I know how to pick 'em!" RJ exclaimed with a grin. "They don't call me the best for nothing. This is gonna mean good things for you. I hope you know that."

In the time it took him to waggle his eyebrows at the end of his sentence, Julie and Angelique left together for lunch. I heard their heels clattering as they ran down the stairs, and I tried to convince myself they weren't running away from me.

"Hey, RJ," I said. "Where do people go for lunch around here?"

"Around here?" he said. "Nowhere unless you've got a car. I'd take you, but I have a meeting. There are some take-out menus over there. Why don't you order yourself a sub?"

And with that, he left too, already yelling into his cell as he loped into the stairwell. The door slammed shut behind him and I was alone.

I shrugged it off. What did I expect? A red carpet welcome? A banquet? I was too stressed to eat anyway. I decided to work on my break moves instead. Nadine would have been proud.

In the afternoon, we were going to meet with the choreographer. I was surprised. Happy, but surprised. I had thought that would come later. Like, after we had actual songs or something.

But RJ said, "Music is all about image, Alya. And the image of EnChantay is three hot chicks who move as hot as they sound. Hell, you can't even hear the music when you have the TV on mute. Naw. The minute the first video for the first EnChantay single drops—which will be June 4 at 3:30 p.m., debuting at number thirty-five in Canada and urban markets in the northeast U.S.—I want every little girl copying the choreography. I want to sell out arenas before you've ever performed live. I want—"

Julie sighed loudly enough to be heard from behind her pillar.

"I want the world for you girls," he finished. "And you're going to give it to me. Right? *Riiight?*"

"Whoo!" said Angelique, pumping her fist. "Hell, yeah!"

"I'm going to go change," said Julie, turning her ever-elegant, forever-pissed-off self towards the change room, where she would no doubt change into a different black outfit, almost indistinguishable from the one she was already wearing.

"Thanks so much for helping me this morning!" I said, following her into the change room, intent on cracking through her crusty exterior. No one could really be *that* mad *all* of the time.

"Don't thank me—I'm doing it for the paycheque," she said.

Okaaay . . . at least she was honest. That was . . . refreshing.

"I'm just excited to be here," I said, realizing instantly that it was exactly the wrong thing to say. Julie turned and glared at me like she'd vaporize me on the spot if her eyes had lasers.

"Have you been in a lot of groups before this one?" I asked.

"I play in a few bands," she said. "Real bands, with real music—not this booty-shaking stuff."

"Well, I'm so happy to finally meet you. I'm sure I have a lot to learn—"

"Oh yes, it's thrilling, I can tell," she said, stepping into a stall and pulling the curtain closed behind her. "Give it time. You'll probably crack like the rest of them."

I laughed it off—a little too loudly, maybe. "I'm not going to quit," I said.

"We'll see," she called back.

Angelique came into the change room.

"So," I asked her, "do rehearsals always go like this—singing in the morning and dancing in the afternoon?"

"No, we're just starting the dancing today. The choreographer wasn't available before," she said, stripping right down to her underwear without even turning her back. Her skin was flawless, her stomach soft but flat, navel pierced, breasts pushed up as high as modern elastic technology would allow.

"Great," I said, trying not to stare, suddenly self-conscious about my A-cup breasts and gangly legs. "At least that's one thing I won't be behind on!" Suddenly my skin felt too dark, my posture too timid, and my sports bra too practical. "Who is the choreographer?" I asked.

"I dunno. Some guy. Raykee? Raffo someone?" Angelique stared back at me, boldly sizing me up.

"Raquo?" I asked, feeling myself shrinking under her stare. I reached for my T-shirt.

"Yeah, Raquo. Whatever."

"He choreographed and directed Bershawn Sera's last video!" I said, pulling my T-shirt on and getting it stuck on my hair, so I was trapped, blind, with my arms over my head.

"Oh right, *that,*" said Angelique. Julie laughed.

"You didn't like it?" I asked, finally righting my shirt and pulling on my track pants. The memory of twenty magnificently toned and cut dancers with glistening abs dancing on orange cars in blue light in the rain replayed in my mind.

Rev it up, you can drive me downtown
Rev it up, you can drive me downtown
Octane, pump-it,
I'm running on fumes
Babe!

"What's not to like?"

Julie laughed. "Angelique's just mad because she met Mr. Sera at a party and he wasn't interested in her."

"Or anyone *like* me," said Angelique. "He was a little too into his 'friends,' if you know what I mean."

I didn't.

"I think I've already said too much," she said. "I'd hate for you to have to re-poster your bedroom or something."

They both laughed.

"Maybe we'll tell you when you're *older,*" said Julie, laughing again. It felt like I was back at RHS.

"All right, I'll see you on the floor, then," I said, forcing perkiness. They kept laughing.

When I stepped back into the studio, standing in the centre of the room was a small man dressed all in grey, from the cuffs of his loose yoga pantaloons to the top of his knit fisherman hat. His arms were crossed over his cardigan, and he was staring down at his soft-soled jazz shoes with intense concentration.

Instinct told me not to disturb him. I tiptoed across the room, trying to sneak a look at his face, and started some quiet stretching exercises, even though I was already pretty warm from my "lunch."

Julie and Angelique emerged from the change room a few minutes later, their laughter now close to hysterical, but they stopped as soon as they noticed Raquo. They followed my lead, and each found a spot on the floor and started to stretch—Julie stiffly, Angelique reaching in such a way that every twist and lean showcased the curve of her nearly bare back or caused her cleavage to heave beneath her halter top.

Finally, after what seemed like an eternity, the man who could only be Raquo looked up.

"Good morning!" he said, beaming, although it was well after two in the afternoon. "How are we feeling today?"

Julie and Angelique looked at each other for direction.

"Good," I volunteered, deciding he must be talking to us.

"Yeah. Good," the other two mumbled after me.

Raquo smiled again.

"Good? You're *good?* Interesting. Well, I'm inspired, deliberating, hopeful, and coiled for release."

Angelique and Julie exchanged a glance that suggested they were incredulous, worried, and a little indignant, and I immediately regretted my choice of words.

"If you're just 'good,'" continued Raquo, "let's see it in practice. Let's put that to the test."

At that, his arm shot out to the left and the stereo suddenly burst to life.

What followed was a bubbling, flowing, waving tsunami of hip-hop steps, so fluid they almost blended together. Raquo moved like a plant blooming in an aquarium, like a fish fighting to escape the hook, like a message in a bottle, lost at sea. Then he announced: "This is your combo!"

I clapped my hands together. "Awesome!" His choreography was even more amazing up close than on TV. Then I saw the stricken expressions on Angelique's and Julie's faces.

"I don't know what you've been told," Julie stuttered, "but we aren't dancers—only Al—"

"So!" he yelled. "The breakdown!"

Raquo's "breakdown" was *fast.* I was used to having to pick things up quickly in my advanced classes at home, and I had done a few workshops in the city that made my head spin, but this was blistering even beyond that.

"A one a two a three a four, five six seven and eight!" he said. "Got that? Okay, repeat."

It was ugly—a total bloodbath. I muddled my way through, but Julie was almost too stiff to keep up, and Angelique was completely off tempo.

"Enough! Stop!" yelled Raquo the second time around. "You need to understand that this piece of choreography was inspired by the bounty of our planet and the secret worlds at the bottoms of our oceans. Love, it takes many forms, yes?"

We waited for his next instruction.

"YES?" he yelled.

"Yes!" I said hurriedly, almost bursting into a laugh.

"This isn't funny! You!" he snapped at me. "Come here." He pointed to a spot on the floor. "You have it?"

"I think so."

"Demonstrate it. Now."

"Alone?"

"Now!"

I didn't know which I was more afraid of—showing off and failing in front of Angelique and Julie, or disobeying Raquo. Raquo, I decided, and forced myself to concentrate.

The music began again. I waited for the gurgle, then

dropped to the crouch, uncoiled, and tried to feel how each step flowed into the next.

Raquo stopped the music when I was done.

"Sorry," I said. "I know I missed the—"

"No!" he said. "That was much better. The ocean. The mystery. I felt it. The steps—those will come. Those we have time for. What we do not have time for is bland, generic, soulless dancing! Do you understand me?"

I nodded.

"DO YOU UNDERSTAND ME?" he shouted, turning to face Julie and Angelique.

"Yes!" they said, trembling in their sneakers.

"Okay," said Raquo. "Group hug. Good work, dancers."

As he pulled us into his chest, the scent of Angelique's perfume filled my nostrils, and her nails dug into my bare arm.

Nine

Madi was still out with Trevor when I got back to the b&b, which was fine by me because all I wanted was to devour a pizza all by myself and then melt into a long, hot bath. Halfway through the pizza, my back started to cramp up, and I consequently became possibly the first person ever to eat half a pizza *in* the bath. It was a desperate time.

I called my parents around nine: yes, we were having a good time; yes, Madi's cousin's apartment was nice (I described our room at the b&b as if it were the imaginary apartment); yes, I was tired from shopping, and tomorrow we were going for breakfast and then coming straight home. Yes, I would bring back bagels for my dad.

I finished the last of my troubling bio homework just as Madi came home, shortly after ten.

"So?" I asked her before she was even all the way in the door.

"It was a pretty good date," she said, beaming.

"Pretty good or really good?" I asked.

"Really, really good."

She sat down, cross-legged, at the end of my bed. I closed my books.

"Trevor had just finished working, so I met up with him and a bunch of people from his work for lunch," she said.

"Ew! What?" I squeaked. "That's not a date! Why wouldn't he want to do something alone?"

"Don't panic. I think he set it up that way so it would be more casual—you know, not so pressurey and stuff. We didn't spend the whole time with work people," she said. "We were sitting all the way at the end of the table, and he only talked to me the whole time anyway, like his friends weren't even there."

"Aww," I said. "That is kind of sweet."

"Yeah, it was kind of, like, almost special-er in a way, because I could see that even though he *could* have talked to his friends, he *didn't,* so I know he was really actually interested in what I was saying."

"So then?"

"After we ate, all his buddies were going to some street-hockey thing, and they asked if we were coming, and they all made fun of him when he said no, but he didn't seem to mind. He just smiled. And then we walked to the Old Port, but we stopped and sort of shopped without really buying anything along the way."

"Aww!" I said. "All the tourist stuff we never get to do with Infinite! You were doing it!"

She laughed. "Yeah. Kinda. So we walked around, just talking, and there was this free museum day on, so we went into the kids' science museum and pressed all the buttons and laughed at all the exhibits. Did you know he's like this physics expert?"

"I did not know that."

"I quizzed him. He is. So after that, we were hungry—"

"Yeah," I said. "Physics always makes me hungry, too."

She ignored me.

"It was, like, dinner by then anyway, so he took me out for crepes, which sounds like some cheesy idea of a date from TV, but actually it was at this tiny restaurant that was underground and not fancy at all—it was really cheap and it looked like it used to be a Chinese restaurant or something, and omigod, it was so good!"

"Oh, man. Crepes. Why didn't I think of that?" I said, suddenly regretting my pizza. Then again, that would have been hard to manage in the bath.

"Then he walked me back here, and that was my date."

"That's a long date!" I said.

"The time went by so fast! It was, like, one minute it was lunch, next minute it was dark out. I knew you'd be worried if I didn't come back soon."

"Did he kiss you?"

"No."

"Why not?"

"Because *I* kissed *him.*"

"Phew. Was he a good kisser?"

"It was so hot, I could hardly walk up the stairs in a straight line after."

"Whoa."

"Yeah, you know when you kiss a guy, and it's just like, *wow,* and then your head spins a little and you're like, *I need more of that, right now*?"

My heart skipped a beat and then sank. I didn't know. Part of me wondered if I ever would. With the few guys I'd kissed, it had been more like, *Ew,* and then I'd wriggled away, feeling like *I need mouthwash, right now.* I'd been trying to convince myself that kissing itself was the problem, more than *who* I'd been kissing, but—

Madi waved a hand in front of my face. "Al?" she said. "You still with me?"

"Are you going to see him again?" I asked dejectedly.

"I hope so. I just don't know when. He's working this

tour thing around the U.S. He won't even be in the country next month."

"Oh, sad," I said, but my heart wasn't in it anymore. It had retreated to a dark corner where it could only worry about itself.

"But enough about me!" she finally said. "How'd it go with EnChantay?"

"Awful," I said.

"I don't believe you."

"Well, it wasn't all bad. The choreographer is Raquo."

"Omigod, *Raquo?*" said Madi. "As in the 'Bershawn video we danced to fifty times a day in grade seven' Raquo? The, 'I got in trouble for putting his moves in my gym routines' Raquo? How can you be so calm? You have to tell me! What was he like?"

I grinned, betraying the actual lack of calm that was bubbling beneath my exhausted exterior. "He was amazing, obviously, but tough—"

"Obviously!" she finished for me. "Wow." She clasped her hands over her heart, and I swear she actually swooned. "Wow," she said again. "Okay, you know what? I am officially, completely jealous."

"Well, don't be," I said. "Raquo might have been cool, but the other girls who are actually *in* the group? They hate me."

"They do not," she said, shifting back into her best-friend tone of voice. "They just don't know you."

"They think I'm useless," I told her. "They think I'm a talentless piece of ass."

"Well, they're wrong," she said. "Your ass is brimming with talent. You have an *explosively* talented ass."

"Ew!"

"If they tell you you got the job, will you still take it?"

"Yeah. The chance to work with Raquo alone—there's no way I could pass that up."

She hugged me. "I'm so proud of you!" she said. "Jealous, but proud. You're going to be a star!"

"One thing at a time," I said. "I'm not even officially hired yet."

I got the call from RJ four days later—just long enough for me to have come to terms with the idea that he was never going to call, and to have preventatively registered for fast-track summer classes in biology and math, as well as a week-long intensive dance workshop in contemporary hip hop.

"Alyaaa—you're in," said RJ's message, shockingly. "Call me. Let's set up the deets. It's gonna be the hotness. Love, love, love it."

My hands started to shake. I called Madi.

"I told you not to register so early," she said. "You'll never get your deposit back."

"Aren't you even going to congratulate me? I said I got in!"

"Obviously. We always knew you would get in. You always get in."

"Thanks."

But then there were my parents. I figured I'd be looking at fifteen to twenty-five years of community service once they realized that Madi had no cousin in Montreal, and that I'd gone to an audition without telling them.

Dinner at my house was tense that night. I fidgeted all the way through, and when we got to the part where it was my turn to "share," I shovelled a gigantic piece of veggie lasagna into my mouth so I could postpone participation by chewing. It didn't work. My parents waited for me to finish while Devin made fun of me with his eyes, making it hard not to choke.

By the time I finally swallowed, I had attracted even more attention to myself than I was trying to avoid in the first place.

"How was your day?" cued my mom.

"Okay, I guess." I yawned, feigning fatigue, boredom, betraying my lousy secret-keeping capacities. "I slept a bit. A guy from Cap Music called to offer me a part in a new R&B group."

Everyone stopped chewing, and an eerie silence descended over the table. Turns out there is no way to casually break some types of news.

Devin shot me a raised-eyebrows look, like, *How could you not tell me?* I shovelled a gigantic bite of salad into my mouth and surreptitiously sent him an "I just found out today, I swear" glance.

My dad put down his fork.

"This is a surprise," he said, maintaining a steady, even tone of voice.

"Did you audition for this? Why didn't you say anything about it before?" asked my mom, smiling to cover the tension in her voice.

"I didn't think I'd get it," I said with a shrug, oversalting my half-eaten dinner. "I went almost on a dare."

"No need to close doors prematurely," said my dad, warming up. "What is this group all about, exactly?"

Now began the tricky part. If I seemed to be too into it, they'd think I was rushing, and they'd take out the giant parental magnifying glass and try to find a million things wrong with it.

"Well," I said, "it's a new group, with three girls, and it's called EnChantay. It's on a new label called Soul292, which is owned by Cap Records. The guys from Infinite know the producer, RJ, and they say he knows what he's doing. They've worked with him before."

No point dropping the Montreal bomb before they'd had a chance to get to like the idea. Devin narrowed his eyes at me. I dug my toe into his shin under the table—the traditional sign for "Shut it, butthead."

"RJ seems like a real go-getter," I said, employing one of my dad's favourite terms. "Obviously it's still really early, but he seems to think he has the right team to pull off a Grammy win."

"Oh, come on," Devin finally said. "How can he *possibly* know that already?"

"They *knew* before it was even released that Bershawn's last single was going to debut at number twenty-four," I told him, like he was the biggest moron ever. "How do you think they pulled that off? Think about it."

"Well," said my dad, squashing the fight that was about to erupt, "they do seem to have very sophisticated ways of calculating these things these days."

Grammys, you say? I could hear him thinking. I knew how his mind worked. He couldn't help seeing business opportunities everywhere he looked. The wheels were already turning in his head, pumping out spinoff groups, TV shows, merchandise—my face on cups in franchise restaurants across the nation.

"I'd like to talk to this RJ character," said my dad.

"You know," I stalled, hoping to delay that phone call as long as possible—to postpone the inevitable moment when RJ got on the phone and said something weird, "Ender knows him pretty well. They've worked together before."

"Can I have his number, please?" said my dad, holding out his hand.

And then there was everything my dad might say to RJ. The odds of someone saying something deal-breakingly embarrassing were perilously high.

"The choreographer is Raquo. He's, like, *the best,*" I emphasized.

"I'll take that into consideration."

"This is such a good opportunity for me," I continued, trying to build my case.

"Alya. The number," he insisted.

I grudgingly pulled RJ's card from my pocket and slid it across the table.

I sat on my bed after dinner with my French homework on my lap and my door slightly open, straining to listen in on the conversation through the door of my dad's study.

Mumble, mumble, talent. Mumble, mumble, mumble, potential. Mumble, future. Lawyer. Education. Happiness. Percentage.

As I pulled all the nouns and adjectives out of a photocopied movie review, I imagined RJ on the other end of the line, pacing back and forth, gesturing with his hands. But I couldn't quite make out what was going on.

I quietly labelled and translated my words as my mom took over the phone. She speaks so softly, she's particularly hard to listen in on.

She burst out laughing. This was an interesting turn. I had expected something more along the lines of slamming down the phone and launching a police investigation. I put my pencil down and crept to my door, straining to listen, but I still couldn't make out more than every other word—and every other word seemed to be either "Oh" or "RJ."

Finally, the house fell silent. After a few minutes, my dad called me into his office.

"He's quite the character," he said. "He had a lot of good things to say about you."

"When were you going to tell us this job was in Montreal?" said my mother.

"I didn't? Sorry. I guess I forgot."

"You *forgot?* When did you audition for this? Where?"

"The first audition was here. The second one—"

"Was the same weekend you stayed with Madi and her cousin," my mother completed for me.

"Yeah," I said with a shy smile.

"Anything else you're forgetting?" she asked.

"No."

They waited to see if I would crack. I waited to see if they would find the hole in the "Madi's cousin" story.

"What did you decide with RJ?" I asked.

"I don't know, Alya," said my dad. "He talks a good game, but I don't trust his obsequious, self-aggrandizing manner."

I cleared my throat. "Aren't you the one who always says the qualities that make a person successful won't necessarily make him your best friend?"

"Yes . . ." he said cautiously. "But we can't just send you off to Montreal, to people we don't know. Madi's cousin was one thing, but this—"

"If it was Devin," I said, "you wouldn't even have to think about it. You'd just put him on the train and leave him to sort it out."

"Devin," said my mom, "is not our baby girl."

"That makes it worse! Totally sexist! I'm not a baby."

"Devin isn't in high school," said my father.

"Summer vacation is coming," I countered.

"He did say they could record over the summer, when she's out of school anyway," my mother conceded.

"What about your job and your dancing? I didn't spend thousands of dollars on dance classes all these years for you to go and give up so you can chase some hare-brained scheme like this."

"There aren't many classes at the studio all summer anyway, and besides, I *am* dancing in this group. It's why they want me."

"I don't understand why it has to be Montreal," said my dad. "The drinking age is lower—peeler bars on every corner."

"Dad!"

"Wallace, really," said my mother, putting a hand on his arm. "She's not going to hang out at 'peeler bars.'"

"No, she isn't," said my dad.

"If I was a boy—" I started.

He put his foot down. "Alya, we're not going to decide tonight. Now please leave us be so we can talk this over."

And I was banished from the office.

Ten

It took several weeks of negotiating—me with my parents, my parents with RJ, RJ with his "backers"—but eventually they worked something out. I barely understood the details, but it meant I could go, and that's all I cared about at the time. There was money involved—only a little at first, but then more and more in stages after we recorded, released videos, won awards, or sold lots of copies. I wouldn't see any of it right away—it would all go into a trust fund I wouldn't get to touch until I was twenty-five.

I wasn't in it for the money, but however much cash it really meant, it was enough that my parents were going to let me go to Montreal every week for the whole summer.

When they told me at first, it was almost like they were mad about it. There was a lot of "If you ever pull a stunt like this again, you will finish high school at a military academy." And then there was a bit of "Do you have any idea how dangerous it was, running off to an audition with strangers in another city?" And a healthy dose of "All you've done is prove to us that you're not responsible enough to do *anything* on your own." Finally we got into "And to think you wanted to just accept whatever terms RJ was going to offer you! You practically would have been a slave to Capitulation Records."

I listened with my mouth shut, nodding seriously, not sure what was going on, afraid to jinx whatever teeny tiny chance I still had. It seemed, almost down to the last minute, like they weren't going to let me go at all.

But I had to hand it to RJ: he had the gift of being both weird and persuasive at the same time. It had worked on me, and I realized it had worked on my parents when my dad finally broke down and told me:

"That being said, we'd rather help you reach your independence than sit back and watch you rebel like one of those kids who winds up in dreadlocks, squeegeeing cars on Queen Street with a Rottweiler in tow."

"So I can go?" I checked.

"You're going to have to work this like a serious job—probably even harder than you do all year at school," said my mother.

"Because I can go?" I wasn't taking anything for granted. I needed to hear them say it before I would believe it.

"This is only for the summer. RJ knows he has to rearrange his production schedule to get this album, or whatever they're calling them these days, done by Labour Day," said my dad.

My heart started to beat a little faster.

"You are to be back in your uniform, in your seat at Rosewood, on the first day of school in September, and not a day later."

"And you're going to come home every weekend. You're not going there to party."

"Which is a concern because . . . I can go?"

They both frowned.

"You can go."

I leaped up from my seat and jumped around the room. "I can go, I can go, I can go! Thank you! Thank you thank you thank you! EnChantay!" I sang as I ran down the hall to my phone. "EnChantay, EnChantay, EnChantaaaaaay! I can't wait to tell Madi!"

It was going to be the best summer ever.

"This is going to be the worst summer ever," said Madi when I told her. We were jogging. The announcement broke her stride. "You're always leaving me. First Rosewood, now this."

"I'm coming back *every* weekend," I reminded her.

"It won't be the same," she said, recovering her pace, then speeding up.

"I wish you could come with me," I told her, picking up my own pace to stay with her. "You can visit."

"Maybe I should just register for summer school," she said. "It might as well be productive if it's not going to be fun."

"Look at it this way: you'll have an excuse to see Trevor," I persuaded.

"I guess," she said, a smile finally starting to tug at the corners of her mouth. She took off in a sprint and I raced after her.

The minute school let out for the year, I was on a train back to Montreal.

"My brave girl, travelling alone," my dad said, with a glint in his eye as he handed me a bagged dinner and fifty bucks, "just in case."

"Now remember, you're getting *on* at Guildwood station and *off* at Gare Centrale in Montreal."

"Yeah. Thanks, Dad."

"You have the number for the police?"

"9-1-1?"

"And call when you get off in Montreal, so we know you're safe."

"Uh-hunh."

"Call if you need *anything.*"

"YES."

"Wait! You forgot something!" said my mom. "My hug goodbye!"

I rolled my eyes but squeezed her tight.

"Poor, delicate Alya," said Devin, getting impatient at the door. "Are you okay to walk to the car, or do you need me to carry you?"

"Shut. Up."

It was a beautiful sunny day, and I could hardly sit still in the car on my way to the station. I was wearing the brand-new "travelling clothes" my mother had bought me as a good-report-card/end-of-school/not-really-going-away present: a crisp, tailored jacket over a slinky tank, highly mature narrow Bermuda shorts, jewelled strappy black flat sandals that showed off my pedicure, a deep shoulder bag with impressive buckles, and gigantic sunglasses that covered half my face. Rolling my suitcase down the platform, I felt like a total star, even if I was in Economy class instead of Elegance, with no fancy upgrade from Madi.

It wasn't realistic for me to stay at a hotel the whole time I was working with EnChantay, and there was no way my parents were sending me to stay with RJ, like he suggested. Instead, he arranged for me to stay in one of the university dorms that was empty for the summer. My vision of fluffy beds and croissants for breakfast evaporated even as Madi noted how cool it was going to be that I basically got my own apartment for the whole summer, and started making plans for the parties we would have when she visited.

I knew there had to be a catch if my parents had agreed to it, and of course the catch was that it had a midnight curfew, with no guests allowed beyond the lobby, and a stern-looking security guard stationed at the door to enforce it.

RJ met me at the train station and drove me to my cell—I mean, dorm room. It was a six-by-nine-foot concrete rectangle with a twin bed, closet, dresser, small desk, chair, and a non-opening window I could see out of if I stood on my tiptoes. There was a phone on the desk, an antiquated Ethernet port where I could plug in my laptop, and a mirror on the closet door.

"You all good here?" said RJ uncomfortably, looking at his watch.

"Great!" I said.

"I got you booked for a vocal lesson first thing in the morning. I'll give you a wake-up call and pick you up bright and early."

"Cool!" I said, unsure how else to respond.

RJ left, and I sat down on the bed, which made a crinkling sound. "All of this is mine," I said to myself, patting the scratchy blue comforter. I took a deep breath, and it smelled of lemon cleaner, old wood, and the ghosts of all the students who'd lived there before me. I unpacked my suitcase, putting my clothes where their clothes had been. I sat down at the desk and ran my finger over the faded outlines of their old graffiti, and the spots where coffee rings had set and exacto knives had slipped, taking a ding out of the laminate surface. I had a sudden urge to sit down and study something, but instead, I made sure I had my key card and took a walk down the hall to check out the bathroom situation.

With all the students gone for the summer, there wasn't another living soul in the hallway. I couldn't tell if there was even anyone else staying on the floor with me. It was so perfectly quiet, it was almost eerie. The bathrooms were vast and white, like an alien testing lab—or maybe that was just my imagination acting up. Fifteen toilet stalls stretched in one direction, fifteen sinks in the other, and beyond them, a long row of bathtubs with showers, hiding behind white plastic curtains. *Definitely won't have to compete for shower time in the morning,* I noted.

There was a lounge with a couple of couches and a TV, and a kind of half-baked communal kitchen consisting of an oven and a fridge with three feet of counter between them. In the fridge, on the middle shelf, there were a couple of plastic grocery bags containing what looked like Tupperware lunches, and there was a carton of milk and some orange juice on the shelf inside the door, so I guessed there must be at least *one* other human around.

I sat down on the couch and was beginning to fiddle with the TV remote when my phone rang.

Oops. Parents. "Sorry. I'm here, I'm fine," I answered on the first ring.

"We weren't worried," lied my mother. "Is RJ taking good care of you? Are you all settled in?"

"Yeah," I said. "Got everything I need."

"Are you sure?"

"Yeah," I said. "Just checking out the kitchen now."

"And you have your meal plan. Don't forget your meal plan."

"Yes, Mom, I'll check out the caf first thing in the morning."

"Alya," she said, "if you have *any* problems, I want you to call me immediately."

"Yeah, Mom."

"Immediately. Do you hear me?"

"Loud and clear."

"You're sure you're okay?"

"Yes! Mom, I'm sure. Geez."

"Okay," she said, like she still wasn't convinced. "I'll talk to you tomorrow."

"Okay. Bye, Mom."

"Love you."

I hung up and walked back to my room, trying to see if I could make my steps match the silence of the hall. I felt almost guilty at the click my door lock made as it slid open to let me into my room again. The AC was blasting. I turned it down. Tired, I climbed into my softest pyjamas, crawled into bed beneath my starchy sheets, and fell fast asleep.

Eleven

The phone on my desk rang at 8:00 a.m. sharp.

"RISE AND SHINE, PHAT AL. WE'VE GOT A BUSY DAY AHEAD OF US!" RJ shouted.

I moaned and rubbed my eyes.

"Geez, kid," he said in a normal voice. "What's wrong with you? You're *young*. Where's your *energy?*"

"Hunh?" I said. No one has ever accused me of being a morning person.

"Ha haaaa," he laughed. "Be downstairs in an hour. We gotta make tracks."

I made RJ stop the cab so I could get a coffee and something to eat at the corner store—sorry, *dep ("DEP, dépanneur, it's DEP. You're in Montreal now, Phat Al, and we call them deps!")*—so we got to the lesson five minutes late.

I didn't realize we had to go all the way across town, and in traffic, too. The classes were based out of the teacher's home in Westmount—a cottagey little house with beams and stone that looked more like something from a storybook than "a place where stars go to become—what's the word for a really big star? Supernova? Are you sure? That sounds so dorky. Whatever. Hot. Where stars go to become hot. I love it!" (RJ's words, not mine.)

I rang the doorbell and it chimed inside—one of those singsong chimes that just wouldn't settle for being any old bell or buzzer. When the door swung open, I was greeted by a woman older than my parents but younger than my grandparents, with golden skin and elegant clothes. Short, wispy hair framed her face, and a pair of delicate reading glasses hung from a gold chain around her neck.

Her name was Davina Deene. She had sung backup for over thirty years, for everyone from Luther Vandross to Shania Twain. RJ had given me some solo jazz CD of hers, but it was still in its shrink wrap, on top of my suitcase.

"Call me Dee," she said, holding out a warm hand.

I slipped off my sandals and followed her up her off-white carpeted stairs to the music room.

"I'm having tea, darling," she said. "Can I offer you a cup?"

"Sure," I said, to be polite, although I'd never been much of a tea drinker.

She left to get the tea, and I teetered on the edge of a stool near the baby grand piano, unsure whether it would be impolite to actually sit, although there was an inviting couch and a reading chair just on the other side of the room. The carpet was plush under my bare feet, and the whole place was decorated in inviting creamy tones. A sleeping cat was curled up on the reading chair, opposite an old fireplace. The area above the mantel was covered in cards and photos and scraps of old show flyers.

I crossed the room to get a better look.

"Dee, all my love, J.T.," said a thank-you card.

"To Dee: The only thing bigger than your voice is your heart!" I couldn't make out the signature. A small Polaroid of Bono giving her a kiss on the cheek was casually tucked behind the card.

At the centre of everything was a large poster from a

Broadway show, *Keeping It Billie!* A younger Dee struck a pose at the centre, and the whole cast had signed birthday wishes around her.

And then, in one corner, where I almost missed it: a snapshot of Dee hugging a really young Bershawn, who was grinning into the camera with his first Juno Award in his left hand. Then another one of him with two Grammys and Dee. And one of him performing at the GruvTV Awards, taken from backstage.

I looked back over all the notes and photos, and my brain struggled to come to terms with what I was looking at. Dee was obviously a *huge* deal. What was *I* doing in the music room of someone who had handwritten notes from three Beatles and had apparently known Bershawn since he was in diapers? Was I even really standing here? Or was I hallucinating? How was I supposed to go through with this lesson?

I stared again at each of the Bershawn photos. He was smiling in every shot, but there was something sad about them, too. I couldn't quite put my finger on it.

"I can't lie. He's my favourite student," said Dee, coming back into the room. I jumped about a foot and a half.

"I'm sorry! I didn't mean to snoop."

"Of course not," said Dee, putting the tea down. "That wall is my pride and joy—my fire. The music is one thing, but it's the people who make it all worthwhile."

"How long have you—?"

"I've been working with Bershawn since he was about sixteen," she said. "I know all the biographies call him a natural, but even nature can use a boost from someone like Davina Deene from time to time." She smiled.

"I'm sixteen!" I blurted like a dork.

Dee smiled. "How about we get started with our lesson now?"

"I'm sorry," I started, without really knowing what I was apologizing for—overenthusiasm, liking Bershawn too much, being an impostor in a world that was obviously far, far cooler than I would ever be.

Dee dismissed my apology with a wave of her hand. "Maybe I can show you some more of my photos sometime," she said, taking a seat at the piano, "but for now, the music."

I nodded and tried to get a grip.

"I don't know what they've taught you already, so why don't we start at the beginning and see what happens?"

Oh god, I thought, *more breathing.* And I was right, but with Dee it was different. For one thing, it felt good—like yoga. For another, when she needed to demonstrate something, she got right down on the floor—in her nice pants and everything—and did it along with me.

My life is really, really weird, I thought to myself at one point, lying on my back, with Davina Deene, vocal coach to the stars, crouched over me helping me feel the difference between breathing into my chest and breathing into my belly.

After that, she got me started on singing right away, moving through scales, just making "aa" or "ee" sounds. There is a lot of room for error in those two little vowels. But Dee's corrections were like poetry.

"Try to imagine," she would say with a sweep of her arm, "that your breath is the river, and your voice a boat. The boat floats on the river, and the river carries the boat forward."

After the killer vowels, we moved on to a weird exercise where I had to try to say "la" clearly with my tongue tucked in behind my teeth. (Hellooo . . . not possible. It came out *ya, ya, ya.*)

And then, she looked up at me and said, "So what song are we going to work on?"

I froze. I hadn't chosen a song. I'd assumed Dee would know something about what I was supposed to be working on.

"RJ didn't tell me what I should sing," I said.

"Oh, I know," said Dee. "We'll get around to working on EnChantay songs eventually, but for now, what's a song that you *like?* Vocal exercises can teach you only so much; you need to sing *songs,* so we should take advantage of the time we have to work on something fun."

"I know Bershawn's 'Mean the World,'" I said sheepishly, remembering how RJ had hated it at my audition.

But Dee just said, "Wonderful! I think we can work with that," and I smiled, feeling like I'd just pulled a fast one on her.

"It's so refreshing," said Dee at the end of the lesson, "to work with someone whose voice is so free!"

"You mean rough?" I asked her.

"Don't be hard on yourself," she said. "It's counterproductive. Your voice is raw, but even rawness has a beauty—like a smooth block of marble. We can chisel away like a sculptor. You have no bad habits for me to train you out of, that's the main thing. Does a sculptor want to start with a piece of rock that some other sculptor has already had his way with? No. It's no small thing to be young and new and open."

Twelve

My lesson with Dee put me in such a good mood that I was still smiling when I arrived at the studio later that morning.

"Good morning!" I sang, crossing the room with a flourish. Angelique and Julie were sitting behind the pillar with their heads bowed over the table. They didn't look up from whatever it was they were reading.

"Hey, guys," I said again. "What's that?"

Julie huffed like the question was tiresome. Angelique snickered. Great. I'd been there thirty seconds and we were already on one another's nerves. Them versus me—a clique of two.

"Final lyrics for our first single," Julie eventually mumbled, handing me a sheet without looking up.

RJ bounded into the studio then. "All right!" he yelled. "This is hot! You're going to love this! After many, *many* trial runs and revisions," he said, looking squarely at Julie, "we *finally* have both the beat *and* the lyrics for the *hit* EnChantay debut single that we're going to start with first."

I looked down at my sheet and read the song title off the top of the page: "Steppin' Out (Girl Fight)."

"This is a different song than the one from the audition," I observed.

"Yesterday's news, baby," said RJ. "This is the new hotness. I want you to memorize these words and inhale this beat through your ears. Get used to the song, make the song your best friend, because this is the song we're going to be working on this week, and for many weeks to come."

"Like we haven't heard *that* before," said Julie, under her breath.

"No!" said RJ. "This time I'm serious. I've booked you guys to open for L'Armée du Funk next month."

Julie's eyes widened.

"I thought they were in Europe!" said Angelique.

"They are. But next month they're performing at Club Gauche, and so are you."

Angelique and Julie began to chatter excitedly over each other.

"But they're huge!"

"Weren't they just on tour with Helicopter?"

"Our *first* show has to be this big?"

"Yeah," said RJ. "'Cause that's what EnChantay is about: big, big, big! But don't panic. It's not a whole set you're doing—just one song. We're just giving people a *taste* of what's to come, not a whole meal, you dig? L'Armée is doing us a favour. I don't want to let them down—or our backers, who will be there, by the way."

Angelique and Julie looked quiet and serious.

"That's right," said RJ. "It's going to be a big night, and we don't have forever to pull it together. So listen up. I give you: your song."

RJ pressed Play and a whooshing, spacey sound filled the room, then a drum pattern like a heartbeat kicked in.

"You guys are going to talk a bit over this intro," RJ yelled. "Get people hyped up a bit for the hotness of the song! The people like the hype!"

An electronic shooting sound came on over the drums, then some agitated strings, and finally, hand claps.

"This is where the vocals start for real!" RJ yelled. "We'll probably accent the chorus with, like, a car horn or a siren or something, to, you know, keep it intense! Nervy! And feedback. And noise. We should add some feedback and noise somewhere. We'll worry about that later."

As the beat looped, I read over the lyrics.

ANGELIQUE:
So you got this man, and you think it's forever.
Your love is real. Break it up? No way, never.
You'll be together for the rest of your lives.
But I got bad news, girl—you better think twice.

JULIE:
Don't talk like that. What you know 'bout my guy?
My boo loves me from the Earth to the sky.
You're up in my face, diggin' into my business.
You better make your point. Stop being foolish.

ANGELIQUE:
He's steppin' out wit'out you.
So tell me, girl. Watcha gonna do?

JULIE:
Not telling you jack, with that mouth full of lies.
Thought we were friends, but you just wanna fight.

ALYA:
Hey yo! Whoa, whoa, whoa, whoa! Don't go getting nasty.
I know it hurts real bad, but let's keep it classy.

ANGELIQUE:
See? That's what she does, 'cause she can't face the truth.

ALYA:
When you tell her like that, you come off soundin' rude.

JULIE:
My guy is true to me. It's you I can't trust.

ALYA:
Naw, she's got your back, girl. Let's have a group hug.

A sinking feeling came over me as I realized that our lead single was going to be about the three of us fighting—and not just fighting like we were actually fighting in life, but fighting over some nonexistent dude. It was what Madi would have called "not exactly feminist literature, hon." I scanned it again for bright spots. I only had four lines. That was a relief. I could get through four lines. And of the three of us, I got to be the peacekeeper—the one who brought the group together at the end. That suited me. I wouldn't have wanted to be the smug friend any more than the jilted one.

I didn't realize I was frowning until Angelique hissed at me, "What's the matter, Alya? Shocked you only have four lines? Jealous much?"

"Angie!" said Julie, but then she started to cough like she was struggling to hold back a laugh.

RJ stopped the beat. "Hey!" he said. "Ladies, please. This is a group effort. There are no stars here. Everyone has an important role to play. No part is small. No line is unimportant."

"I know!" I said. "I wasn't—" I stopped myself, pretty sure that telling them I didn't like the song would actually be worse. "I love my four lines," I finished quietly.

Angelique kissed her teeth. Julie rolled her eyes.

"Let's listen again," said RJ, "with our ears this time, like professionals."

Lunch that day started out like a replay of my trial weekend in May. No sooner had the long hand hit twelve than Julie and Angelique grabbed their bags and hightailed it to the stairs.

But then RJ stepped between them and the door. "Not so fast!" he said.

Angelique pouted. "What?"

"Aren't you forgetting something?"

Julie furrowed her brow. "I don't think so."

Not too subtly, he gestured at me with a tilt of his head.

"Oh . . ." said Julie. "I . . ."

"Huh?" said Angelique, feigning confusion. RJ crossed his arms over his chest.

"Fine," said Julie, then she turned to me sweetly—or mock-sweetly. "Sorry, Alya, I'm so used to it being just the two of us. I didn't think. We're going to Lucie Laittue for lunch. Want to come?"

"Sure." I shrugged like it was no big deal.

Julie's car was a beat-up old grey Focus. I rode in the cramped back seat with my knees up around my ears, next to a mountain of cables, binders, clothes, and old water bottles, while Angelique helped herself to the front passenger seat and all its leg room. Julie drove like she was used to rushing everywhere, alternately speeding and slamming on the breaks.

"When you have to play in five bands to pay your

rent, you'll drive like this too," she said without taking her eyes off the road.

"Five bands!" I said. "Wow."

"Music is what I do," she said seriously.

We raced through several blocks of dead nowhere neighbourhood before finally surfacing in a 'hood Nadine would have liked—kind of bumping, with restaurants and stuff, but grimy enough to be "real."

"What about you, Angelique? Do you play in other bands?"

"No. EnChantay is my focus. It has 100 percent of my attention," she said, primly.

"You don't have another job?" I asked.

"No," she snapped. "Nothing important."

"I think it's smart to keep another job," I said. "At least until the album drops."

Angelique didn't say anything.

We went into the restaurant, ordered at the counter, and then grabbed a table by the window. Julie and Angelique stared at each other across the table like they were trying to communicate using only their eyes, so they wouldn't have to talk to me.

"So!" I said, with forced energy. "What did you guys do before EnChantay? How did you end up here?" I would get them talking somehow. I was determined.

Angelique cracked first. I was surprised, but then again, I had just offered up her favourite topic of conversation: herself.

"This is my dream," she said. "This is what I've always wanted to do. That's why I left school as soon as I could—to work and perform and get myself out there. I have to strike while I'm in my prime."

I nodded. "What about you?" I asked Julie.

"I studied classical music and jazz for a long time. Vocals and keys and anything else different people need."

"She's been at it *forever,*" said Ange, with a flicker of mischief. "Our girl Julie is OLD."

"Twenty-seven is not *old,*" said Julie. "Besides, everyone's going to look old to Alya. She's younger than sperm."

Angelique laughed. "What grade are you in, Alya?"

"Twelve," I lied. "But, like, only because I was held back a year."

"So that would make you . . . eighteen?" said Ange, grinning. "You lie. *I'm* eighteen." She fixed her green-gold eyes on me. It was like being caught in a tractor beam. My mouth went dry.

"*You're* eighteen, Angie?" said Julie. "And you've been bartending for how long? I may be older, but at least all my jobs have always been music."

Anger flashed in Angelique's eyes and she opened her mouth like she was about to yell, but then our food came, and her attention shifted.

While I tucked into my chili, Julie patted the grease off her fries with her napkin, and Angelique picked all the croutons off her salad and set the dressing aside.

"So, do you guys live nearby?" I asked them.

"No," said Julie. "I live in Montreal North."

"With her mother," snorted Angelique. All bets were off now.

"And *she* lives in a slum apartment with three roommates," said Julie.

"Two roommates," Angelique corrected. "And it's not a slum. It's *Plateau-adjacent.* It has exposed brick *and* a dishwasher."

"Anyway, there's no EnChantay Loft in Old Montreal, if that's what you were wondering," Julie clarified. "This isn't an episode of *Star Pads*. And by the way, I own my apartment, and my mother pays me rent."

"Cool," I said. "Great."

And then we finished our lunch in tense silence—Angelique and Julie glaring at each other between bites, me holding my tongue, afraid I would incite World War Three if I asked them about their favourite movies or where the good shopping was.

I called Madi from the lounge that night while I simmered a totally student-like dinner of beans and rice. The caf was always closed when I got back to the dorm, and I had already figured out my allowance would never last if I ate out every day.

Madi listened intently as I described my day.

"What we need to do," she said, "is dig up as much dirt on the other girls as possible, to even out the playing field. What are their names again?"

"Hang on," I said, opening my own laptop and starting a search. Eight seconds later, I had found Julie's PopLife profile. I sent her the link.

"Wow," said Madi. "This girl is boring."

Julie only had about eighty "friends," and her profile was locked down so hard, we couldn't even see any photos beyond her profile headshot, which was just her, smiling, in a nice sweater. Someone's arm was around her, but she'd cut him out of the photo.

"Maybe she's just really private," I suggested. "She seems really focused on work. I think she's, like, *always* working. She's in five bands."

"Whoa," said Madi.

I searched again, and found she was a regular commenter on MontrealGigs.com—mainly to promote her own shows. From the looks of things, she played three or four instruments on top of singing (if tambourine counts as an instrument?).

The only other place she showed up online was in a local news story about community violence, where she was quoted as saying, "More education is needed for youth and police alike."

"Ho. Hum," sang Madi.

"Well, try finding Angelique, then," I said.

"What did you say her last name was?"

"Fielleux."

"Aha!" she said. "Does this AngieF look familiar to you?"

I clicked the link she sent me, and Ange popped up on my monitor, wearing a bright-orange V-neck tee that said "Dynamite Comes in Small Packages" and batting her eyelashes into a camera she was no doubt holding herself, the shot cunningly angled to include an eyeful of cleavage.

"That would be her," I said.

"And her profile is set on public!" said Madi.

"Whoa!" I said, as a screen of photos opened up. "Photo 1 of 530 of AngieF."

Angelique was obviously not spending her evenings locked in her room, reading. There she was with her friends at some club, posing for photos; with her friends at a house party, posing for photos; with her friends shopping—and posing for photos. She did it so much, she even had signature poses.

Pose 1: Turned slightly away from the camera, one foot in front of the other, opposite arm up in the air, excited expression.

Pose 2: Turned slightly away from the camera, one foot in front of the other, hands on hips, knowing smile.

Pose 3: Standing on one foot, other knee bent with her foot behind her, blowing a kiss at the camera.

"What are we supposed to be getting out of all of this?" I asked Madi, starting to feel like some kind of stalker.

"I don't know yet," she said. "But I figure if you're supposed to keep your friends close and your enemies closer, you might as well keep tabs on everyone until you know who is who."

"They're not enemies. They're just . . . difficult."

"Ooh!" she said. "Look! This page lists all these commercials she acted in as a kid—cereal, detergent, three different Barbies!"

I closed the window. "I think I'd rather get to know them the conventional way, if that's okay with you."

She sighed, disappointed. "We were just getting on a roll."

"Madi—"

"Fine."

I hung up and ate my dinner while flipping through meaningless reruns and this one really weird mini-golf show on TV. Eventually I came to hate what was on every single channel, and I turned it off. I did my dishes slowly, half hoping someone would come into the lounge, straining to hear a door open or the elevator ding. But no one came.

Walking back down the hall to my room, I was overwhelmed again by the crazy silence of the place. I flopped down on my bed and turned Bershawn on loud and contemplated the pinprick pattern in the ceiling tiles. I even, for the briefest moment, considered calling my mother and pulling the kill switch—telling her that I was going crazy, that no one really wanted me here, that the highlight of my whole day had been Madi and a sad pot of brown rice, and that I wanted to come home right now and forget the whole thing.

But I couldn't let myself do it. Not after day one. Not knowing how many girls had come before me and dropped out. I didn't want to be just another one of them.

"Arrrgh!" I yelled at the ceiling, over Bershawn.

Then I got up and did what anyone in my family would do: I baked (from a mix I'd bought at the dep, yes, which I knew was deeply, fundamentally wrong, but I tried to make amends by adding extra vanilla, chocolate chips, and a pinch of cinnamon and spice).

It was a little awkward in that tiny lounge kitchen, using a pot as a bowl and an aluminum takeout container as a pan, but as I mixed the batter and set the timer so the brownies would be just fudgy enough—not too cakey and not too soft, either—I started to feel a little better. By the time the timer went off and the brownies were cooling on the counter, I had persuaded myself that tomorrow would be a better day.

Thirteen

But the next morning brought only the same song with fresh horrors. And first, I had to make it worse with my stupid brownies.

Julie and Angelique peered at them like they might leap out of the pan and attack them.

"They're low-fat," I explained. Then it happened.

"You think we're fat?" said Angelique.

"No," I said. "I just always make them low-fat, and since you ordered low-fat stuff at the restaurant yesterday—"

"I'm off wheat," said Julie.

"I don't eat breakfast," said Angelique.

RJ burst into the studio. "All right, ladies, let's make magic!" he yelled. "We've got the group, we've got the song, the backer is giving us four weeks to give him results, so let's blow his mind. Whaddya say? Are we hot? Do you love it?"

"I still think four weeks is too tight," said Julie, her jaw tightening with stress.

"I know you'll deliver," said RJ.

Of course, it was easy for him to be confident. *He* wasn't going to make the magic; Julie was. Like Cinderella, she was always there in the morning when I showed up, and still there at night when I went home. Any time there was a problem with lyrics or music, or anything at all, RJ barked at Julie to take care of it, and she did. She never took breaks, never smiled, and rarely complained. Was this the job she had signed on for, or was she simply working to prove herself, hoping to get something more out of it, kind of like me?

"Whoa, brownies? Awesome!" said RJ, sitting down heavily on a stool in the corner. "Just pretend I'm not here," he said through a mouthful of chocolate.

Julie rolled her eyes. "Let's start," she said crisply, sitting down at the piano. "We have a lot to get through."

I nodded, nervous. It was one thing to run through exercises with Julie or Dee, but this was a real song—a hit single, unless I, Phat Al, ruined it. The feeling of RJ's eyes on the back of my neck only made it harder to focus.

Julie lifted her hands and began to play. Angelique closed her eyes and began to rock back and forth with the beat like she was alone in the room. She took a deep breath, opened her mouth wide, and sang:

"*So-o-o-o-o-o-o-o-o-o-o—*" she began, pressing her fingers to her left ear and squinting as she concentrated.

I was surprised. Her voice was airy and light. It wasn't the strong one I had heard on the audition tape—that must have been Julie. Even as it rose and fell through her interpretation of "so," twisting and turning, flipping somersaults around the notes, it was light and breathy. But she looked perfect doing it: eyes closed, head back, lip gloss glistening. It took effort not to stare.

Julie lifted her hands off the keys. "Angie, stop. What was that?"

Angelique looked confused. "What?"

"It's *so*. Not *so-o-o-o-o-o-o-o-o-o-o-o.*"

"I'm adding my personal style, so it's not so blah."

Julie turned to RJ. He turned away and looked out the window. She pursed her lips together. "We don't have thirteen counts for your personal style right there. The word is *so.* You have to sing *so.*"

"*So-o-o—*" she started again.

"*So,*" said Julie.

"*So-ow—*" sang Angelique.

"*So.*"

"This is how I *sing,*" said Angelique. "It's my gift. RJ, tell her how you told me this is how you want me to sing it."

RJ just laughed, shook his head, and bit into a second brownie. "Alya, by the way, these are fantastic. Keep it up and I'm giving you your bonus early, ha haaaa."

Julie made a sound that was somewhere between a huff and a low growl. "Let me put it this way," she said to Angelique. "I know you can sing it big. You know you can sing it big. RJ knows you can sing it big. There'll be lots of places for you to sing it big. But if you start that big, there's not going to be any room for it to grow. Don't unwrap your gift three days before your birthday. Save it. Allow everyone to enjoy the pretty wrapping paper and the bows and the glitter while the anticipation builds, so the surprise—the bigness—will feel that much bigger."

"Julie!" RJ exclaimed, crumbs flying everywhere. "That was beautiful."

Angelique's nose crinkled like she might cry, but then she took a deep breath, shook out her whole body, starting with her hands and ending with her hair, and sang:

"*So-o-o-o!*"

"Close," said Julie. "That was very close."

RJ applauded. "Now that's teamwork! So hot! I so love it!"

It took an hour to get through the first two verses. It was starting to look like we might not get to my part before lunch when RJ finally barked my name, startling me out of a daydream that I would never have to sing at all—that they would decide to keep me on as a video dancer, and we could forget that EnChantay was ever supposed to be a trio, and they could just rework the song somehow so I wasn't on it.

"Alya! You missed your cue. Not hot."

"Sorry," I said.

"Don't be sorry. Be on time."

Julie took it back to a few lines before: *"Not telling you jack, with that mouth full of lies. Thought we were friends, but you just wanna fight."*

I heard the spot where I was supposed to come in, but when I opened my mouth, I hesitated.

"What are you waiting for? Permission?" asked Julie.

"No, I—"

Angelique snickered like she wasn't learning the song at ten minutes a word herself. "Maybe you should write her a hall pass, RJ," she said.

"I'll count you in. Julie, take your last line again. Alya, you come in on one."

My cheeks burned. I knew how to count to one. It wasn't hard; it was just— *Enough,* I told myself. No more excuses. Just get it right this time.

"Thought we were friends, but you just wanna fight," sang Julie.

"Five, six, seven, eight, ONE," counted RJ.

"Hey yo! Whoa, whoa, whoa, whoa! Don't go getting nasty," I sang, on time, but so tentatively I could barely hear myself. RJ made a clicking sound with the tip of his tongue.

Julie lifted her hands from the piano. "Okay, that was better. But let's think about that line for a minute. '*Hey yo! Whoa, whoa, whoa, whoa!*' It's strong. You're *interrupting.* You can't be singing it like you're waiting for someone to tell you it's okay. You're stepping in to break up a fight. *Excuse me, may I interrupt you?* is not going to work.

"*I* could sing it. *I* can do big," said Angelique, puffing out her chest.

"RJ," said Julie, "how would you feel about giving Alya all of Angie's verses so that Angie can sing this line?"

Angelique tossed her hair. "That's not what I meant. You know it should be a duet anyway."

I gritted my teeth and tried to get a grip. When I was dancing, I never cared who was watching me or what they were thinking. I just danced. I performed. *This is no different,* I told myself. *Be professional.*

We tried it again. "*Hey yo! Whoa, whoa, whoa, whoa!*" Julie didn't stop me. It was a breakthrough. "*Don't go getting nasty,*" I continued. "*I know it hurts real bad, but let's keep it classy.*"

"*See? That's what she does,*" Angelique sang right at me, like we were really having a conversation. It was spooky how she looked at me like she believed every word she was saying.

"Good!" Julie yelled over her. "Good!" Then she sang her line. "*My guy is true to me. It's you I can't trust.*"

This time I didn't waste my moment.

"*Naw,*" I almost shouted, putting as much fighting energy as I could into it. "*She's got your back, girl!*" It felt good. It felt natural. As I got to the end of the verse—"*Let's have a group hug*—" I realized that while Julie was running the show and Angelique had the biggest part, *I* had the most important line in the song. *I* was the only one who could convince them to stop fighting—to make sure everyone would be friends. Mine was the last voice anyone would hear before we went back into the chorus.

So I dug deep and pushed aside my nerves, and I put everything I had into that "*hug.*" I closed my eyes and pictured everything a hug meant, and I tried to make it warm, embracing—the hug to end all hugs. It started out deep, then I squeezed it in the middle, before finally letting it go gently, releasing it back into the song.

When I opened my eyes, Julie and Angelique were both staring at me, wide-eyed. RJ had his hand over his mouth. They exchanged a three-way look that said *I didn't know she could do that.* I nodded a small thank-you as Angelique dove into her last trip through the chorus.

That's when I understood it—the magic RJ was talking about.

Angelique ended with a final, triumphant, improvised *"Oh, it's fo sure that I know,"* and it was all I could do to keep myself from clapping. I did clap.

"Whew!" I exclaimed. "Omigod, you guys! That was amazing!"

Julie smiled an inexplicably calm smile.

"Alya's working with Dee now, right, RJ?" she asked.

"Yeah," he answered.

"Good," she said, her voice going flat. "She needs it. Alya, I don't know what that thing was you tried to do on '*hug,*' but I don't ever want to hear it again. Understand?"

"I—" I looked to RJ, confused. He looked to the floor.

"Just sing it straight, Phatski."

"Okay," I said, too embarrassed to even ask what was bad about it.

I hid in the change room until I was sure the rest of them had already left for lunch, then I voluntarily practised b-girl moves and ate my leftovers from the night before, while they went off wherever, no doubt to compare notes and laugh hysterically at my total suckitude.

Fourteen

The next week, to my relief and Julie's dismay, we worked on the choreography more than we did the song.

"Get used to it," I overheard RJ telling Julie. "People will accept whatever we give them as long as the beat is good and you look hot. We've got the beat, so what's missing?"

"We only have three weeks until we put the song on stage, and we're not even dancing when we open for Armée!" Then she lowered her voice. "I know it's only one song, but Angie is out of control, Alya is all over the place. If we only have one chance with this backer—"

"The song is going fine," he said. "The choreography we need for the video. Shooting starts right after the Club Gauche show, remember?"

"But—"

"Thanks, Julie, you're the best," he said, and then he locked himself in his office. She groaned and headed for the change room.

I had been warming up the whole time they'd been talking. No sooner had RJ and Julie left the room than Raquo walked in, catching me mid-transition between two headstand freezes.

"Hey, great!" he said when he saw me. I untangled myself as fast as I could and jumped to my feet.

"Hi, sir," I said, with probably way too much enthusiasm.

He smiled and removed his jacket, but kept his earflap hat on. (He would lead the entire session that way.)

"I appreciate your respect," he said, "but you can call me R."

"Oh, okay. Hi . . . *R,*" I said, blushing a little.

"It's Alya, right?" he checked.

"Alya, Al, Phat Al. Anything really. Well, not A or . . ." I was babbling. "I can't wait to see the rest of the piece."

"The underwater one?" he asked. "I scrapped it. I worked out something new. It's going to blow the old one out of the water. No pun intended."

"Oh."

"Don't look sad. I'm serious. This shit is the shit."

"Okay."

"It's not just 'okay,' Alya," he said. "It's elevating—transformative—it's like going to bed a caterpillar and waking up a butterfly."

It was a *western,* we found out, once Angelique and Julie had surfaced from the change room.

"But not just *any* western," said Raquo. "Its a *vampire* western. It has all the heat of a duel at high noon, only it has to happen at night, or you'll turn to dust." He put his head down for a minute and closed his eyes. "No!" he said, when he looked back up. "You *will* turn to dust. But only at the end."

He magically produced a notebook from his pants and scribbled in it frantically for a solid five minutes until, finally, he looked up again, disoriented.

"Let me show you how it works. Alya, can you get the music?"

"Sure."

"*Sure,*" Angelique mimicked behind me.

"You have something to say, you with the hair?" Raquo snapped.

"No." She glowered at me as the music started.

"So we start with this swaggering walk," Raquo explained. "But we're not swaggering like cowboys; we're swaggering like cold, undead vampires, so we're swaggering stiffly—but sexy stiff, not geriatric stiff.

"It's *important,*" he said, "to pay attention to *detail.* Then—" He leaped halfway across the room, as though actually possessed of supernatural strength. "You, taller one," he said to Julie. "You'll be standing over here, proud, silhouetted in the moonlight, when you notice—" He leaped to the other side of the room. "You with the hair vamp-swagging towards her. And you, Hair, your job is to really put the vamp in vampire."

Why was he calling her Hair? I looked for an opportunity to raise my hand and remind him of their names, but he was speaking so frantically fast, I couldn't get an elbow in edgewise.

"When you reach this point," he continued, "you start your first verse—*So you got this man, and you think it's forever.*" He leaped back to Julie. "You, Tall, react like her words are shattering you—like you can't take the frequency of her voice."

He slowly bent backwards until he was practically folded in two at the knees, his body stiff as a board, perpendicular to the floor.

"I don't know if I can *do*—" Julie started to say.

"Shh! I'm demonstrating."

He fell flat to the ground, arms and legs splayed.

"So you're down," he yelled from the floor, "but you're not out. As you sing—*Don't you talk like that . . . my boo loves me*—you are slowly. Pulling. Yourself. Back. To. Your. Feet. Then, fully standing, you pull out a gun, with one silver bullet."

"That's for werewolves, not vampires," said Angelique.

"She's right," I said, maybe not loudly enough.

"You have a gun, Tall," he said a little louder. "And on *Stop being foolish,* you whip it out." He manufactured a finger gun and brandished it in Angelique's face.

"That is really cool—" I started to say, before I remembered the no-talking rule. Raquo winked at me. Angelique and Julie scowled.

"And that's where we'll stop it for now," he said. "I think that will be plenty to take us to the end of the day."

The rest of the afternoon was spent in "vampswag" boot camp. The move took the simple act of walking with attitude and broke it down into eight different steps. There was a kind of secret logic to it, but it felt as if the top and bottom halves of my body were working against each other. It was like learning to walk all over again.

Angelique and Julie weren't doing so well. Every time Raquo issued a correction, they exchanged a glance and sank farther to the back of the room. That left me alone at the front, which just made me want to nail it that much harder.

"Good, Alya! Everyone, try again," Raquo said. For all his brutality, he was patient, letting us (well, *making* us) run it over and over again.

Julie worked and worked at it, but Angelique just seemed to let her frustration get the better of her, giving up when she couldn't get it on the first try. The more she slouched and sighed at the back of the room, the lazier she looked, the more irritated Raquo became.

"Hair! No!" he yelled, catching her in the act of skipping over some steps that were bothering her. "Heel, not knee!"

Angelique finally lost it. "Look, my name isn't *Hair,* it's—"

"I'll learn your name when you show me why it's worth remembering," he snapped.

I drew in a sharp breath and almost ducked, half-expecting her to whip off her shoe and throw it at his head. But instead she turned calmly and walked to the change room.

"I should go see—" said Julie, turning to follow her, but Raquo called her back.

"Tall! I want to see it again. Alya, excellent. Everyone should do it so well."

I winced at the compliment. Julie grimaced. Raquo watched us run it again with his arms crossed.

At the end of the day, we found Angelique sitting on the floor of the change room with her head in her hands.

"Are you okay?" Julie asked her.

"No, I'm not okay," she said. "That guy—his job is to make us look good, and he gives us this crap that is not only weird but impossible? I'm *never* going to 'vampswag.'"

I felt a pang of sympathy. It wasn't so different from how I felt about singing.

"You're going to get it." I told her. "You just—"

"I don't *just* anything," she said, cutting me off. "Who are you to judge, just because you can do it already?"

The force and anger of her words threw me off balance. "I'm not judging you, Angie, I—"

"*What* did you just call me?" She stood and stepped forward, leaning in until she was an inch from my face. "Ange*lique.* It's *Angelique* to you," she spat.

I stepped back in shock.

"Don't give me that look," she said. "You're lucky I let you call me anything, you insignificant little suck-up."

"Hey!" I finally said, staring her straight in the eye. The deepness of my own voice surprised me. "I wanted to help."

I grabbed my bag and sidestepped her to leave the room. I had to get out of there before she could see that she'd got to me.

Fifteen

It was hard to leave a rehearsal like that and then go back to the empty dorm. By my second week with EnChantay, I had already begun to resent the way that, even though it was practically like living in my own needlessly vast apartment, the institutional bleakness seemed to overpower everything. Even alone, I felt as if I had to tiptoe to the bathroom and look over my shoulder while I watched TV. And despite my loneliness, in those rare times when another person was actually on the floor, I would feel oddly put out. I'd resent the sight of a lunch in the fridge or toothbrush left by one of the many bathroom sinks. There was no comfort in my room, with its hard bed, cold floor, and light switch on the opposite wall from the bed, so I could never fall asleep reading. It felt a little like living at work; none of my time was ever fully my own.

Noticing these things made me feel whiny, and I *hate* whining. But earlier and earlier each week, I began to long for the weekend, when I could go home to my own comfy bedroom with my own fluffy bed and soft sheets, not to mention the Force and my family.

I finally knew for sure I was homesick when I found myself actually missing Devin.

"It just sucks so hard, so much of the time," I told him over the phone one night.

"It's work!" he said. "It's supposed to suck."

I hadn't thought of it that way before. What was that? Actual wisdom? From Devin? Impossible.

On the train home that weekend, I replayed every snide thing Angelique had said to me all week—every huff, every sidelong glance—and there was a lot of time for it. The train took forever just getting out of the station in Montreal. By the time it hit something approaching a reasonable speed, I felt just about ready to leap out the window and run the rest of the way home. I was already sick of the same blue-green upholstery of the seat in front of me and the same flat, shrubby land out the same brown-grey tinted windows. I used to hope someone interesting would sit down next to me, and no one ever did. Then I would hope for no one at all to sit there, so I could stretch out across both seats, but then *someone* always did—either some business dude with earbuds and a laptop or a middle-aged woman with a paperback novel. I had nothing against them, but did they have to be the same two people over and over and over again like that? They were more repetitive than the watery landscape art at the head of each car and the hummus platter from the food cart I was growing to hate. Even the music from my own iPod started to get on my nerves after a while.

If I could have jumped out of my seat, gone for a run, danced it out—anything—maybe I could have shaken it out of my system and found a way to be more positive. But trapped in my seat, I basically spent five hours working my stress over Angelique and Julie into a full-blown obsession. Soon it was all I could think or talk about.

"Do you not remember what the Hydra Force was like in the beginning?" Madi asked at crew practice. "I had to *beg* Nadine to hang out with me."

"Mm-hmm," said Nadine. "And she tricked me into letting you in."

"And then it was like pulling teeth even getting her to *consider* Devin," finished Madi.

"And she *still* thinks I'm a pain in the ass," said Dev.

Nadine threw a cushion at his head.

"See?" he said. "See?"

Madi collapsed out of her shoulder freeze and looked up at me from the floor. "I don't know why you need this Angelique chick to like you anyway. The bitchier she is, the more you're going to want to beat her. It's better for you if she *doesn't* like you. Besides," she continued, a little more timidly, "you already have your real friends right here, right?"

"I'm not supposed to be battling her," I said. "We're supposed to be on the same side."

She sighed and threw herself back into her freeze, hard enough that she overshot it.

And this is where things started to get weird for me: about halfway through each weekend, after twenty-four hours of obsessing over how awful it was, I would start to almost . . . *miss* EnChantay somehow? Working with Dee would have been the highlight of my week, no matter what I had to put up with to do it. And I looked forward to Raquo's sessions at least as much as I feared them. And even if it meant waking up in that dorm, I liked the feeling of getting up in the morning and going to work, dancing, singing—performing with my whole body, my brain, and my heart—even if all three of them took a serious beating on alternating days. I wanted to be there so badly; I hated being there so much. It made me sound crazy. It made me feel crazy. I didn't like crazy. Crazy was Nadine territory, or Madi even, but not me. I was Phat

Al, not Crazy Al. Phat Al was going to conquer the world someday. Crazy Al sounded like someone who wanted to sell you a stolen stereo.

Once word spread across Rivercrest, things only got weirder. The pressure was fierce. I don't know who'd been blabbing. My parents, I guess, and Madi, maybe? After a week, I couldn't go anywhere without someone asking me whether I was famous yet, or telling me how much ass they hoped I was kicking in Montreal. My parents would greet me at breakfast with "How's my little superstar doing this morning?" Mrs. Chloe, my boss at the Movement Spa, asked me to autograph my headshot on the wall. I didn't know how to tell them I might not even survive July, let alone make it to the lifetime achievement awards.

Even girls from school knew. I guess some news is so big it just spreads itself.

I was grabbing a smoothie with Madi after practice when we ran into Raniya and Gina, who were probably my best friends at Rosewood, if you could call them that, since we never hung out outside of class.

"Oh. My. God. Alya Merchant. In the flesh," said Raniya.

"Whoa!" I said. "What are you guys doing so far east of Yonge Street?"

"We're supervising! Ran won that young entrepreneur's award, so we're running jewellery carts at strategically located shopping centres this summer," said Gina.

"But more importantly, what have *you* been up to?" Raniya asked.

"We've heard rumours," Gina added. They always did that—cut each other off, finished each other's sentences. You needed both of them together to make a complete paragraph.

"I've been working on this band thing."

"Listen to her!" said Raniya. "'Working on this band thing.' So modest. That's not what we heard. We heard you'd been *discovered.*"

"Was it like one of those modelling articles in *Sizzle?* Where the girl's agent is always like, 'I was shopping, and as she walked towards me, carrying that box of tampons, I saw it: star power!'" said Gina, picking up speed as she grew more animated.

"Are you getting paid?"

"Do you hang out with other singers now?"

"Did you meet Bershawn?"

They were yelling over each other, loud enough for anyone to hear. Madi looked back and forth from one to the other, trying to keep up.

"Are the other girls in the group hot?" asked Gina.

"I don't know," I said. "How would I know?" I said, too bitterly.

"Are you going on tour?"

"Will you have a video?"

Raniya clutched my arm for emphasis. "Do you want to hang out next week? How come we never hang out?"

"Rehearsals are in Montreal. I won't even be here," I said.

"Oh," said Gina.

"So . . ." said Raniya, suddenly out of things to say.

"We should probably get going," said Gina. "We have to be at the Eaton Centre by three."

"Good luck with everything!" Raniya said, grabbing Gina's hand.

And they raced together across the parking lot, arm in arm.

"Wait a minute," said Madi. "Are they a . . . couple?"

"Yeah." I said. "Is that a problem?"

"No," she said, looking after them. "That would just be so . . . weird. That's all. I mean, can you imagine?"

"No," I said quickly. "Why would you think I could imagine if you can't?"

"I didn't mean—" she started, her eyebrows coming together quizzically. "Why are you being so—?"

"I'm not. Forget it. I'll race you to the Smoothie Hut," I said suddenly, taking off at a sprint. Nice save.

"No!" she yelled, walking slowly after me.

The distance that widened between us was more than just symbolic.

I logged on to PopLife that night, telling myself I wasn't doing it to see what Angelique and Julie were up to that weekend that was better than what I was doing. But that's the first thing I did. Julie was, as usual, playing three shows and attending a workshop. Angelique—she was everywhere and nowhere. I knew the photos would surface later that night or the next morning, but she only ever let you know what she had *done,* never what she was going to do. I thought that, maybe if I looked hard enough through her profile, I might find something that would tell me what made her tick. But for all the information she'd posted, none of it seemed to add up to anything solid. Her favourite colour was purple, but she didn't like to wear it. Her favourite food was salad—without dressing. She liked to listen to whatever was on the radio as long as it was loud and she could sing along. People left her more comments than she left for them. Someone was always inviting her to something. In at least a third of her photos, she was on her phone. Her interests were "being on stage, singing, fashion, booty-shaking, sky-diving, and 'use your imagination.'"

She had two favourite quotes:

"I won't be happy till I'm famous as God."—Madonna

"If I'd observed the rules, I'd never have gotten anywhere."—Marilyn Monroe

My own page was drab. Madi and I had made fun of Julie's profile, but ours were no more exciting. Even between the two of us, we didn't have as many friends as Angelique. A typical conversation on my comment board went like this: "Yo Al, thanks for the biology notes," "No probs, see you in pre-calc." No matter how brilliant I was in the studio, in school, or in Rivercrest, out in the larger world, in real life, I was a tiny insect to Angelique's towering T-Rex.

Sixteen

On Monday morning, Dee listened patiently as I described my "Girl Fight" humiliation.

"Julie wants me to sing one way, and you want me to sing a different way, and then Angelique is allowed to sing however she wants," I complained. "When I tried to do it her way, since it seems as if that's what RJ likes, I sounded stupid."

Dee waved me off.

"So you tried something, and it didn't work. Now you know you have to keep trying. That's the whole point of rehearsing."

"I don't feel like I'm rehearsing. I feel like I'm guessing. I have no idea what I'm supposed to be doing when I open my mouth in there. Besides, I only have two weeks! Two weeks, and I'm going to be up on stage in front of who knows how many people, not knowing what I'm doing, ruining everything for EnChantay in front of all these important pe—"

"I know it can be confusing at first," said Dee, stopping me, "but we're aiming for two things: one, to develop your technique in order to protect your voice and teach you how to use it as an instrument, and two, to develop *you* into a vocal *performer.*"

"In the next two weeks? Seriously, if I screw it up—"

She held up her hand again.

"It's true. The technique will take time. The only thing for that is patience and practice. But what you can start working on right now, and what I'll want you to keep in mind at all times, is that you always have to sing as yourself. You don't need to put on a special 'singing voice,' different from your speaking voice. You don't need to reproduce the same sound as Angelique, or Bershawn, or anyone else. It won't work, because what is performing?"

I stared back at her blankly. "I don't know." That was a weird thing to admit. After so many years on stage, I'd thought I was an expert.

Dee smiled. "Performing is communication—lending a piece of yourself to your audience. If it doesn't ring true, they see through you. I don't know what RJ wants from Angelique, but if he wanted exactly the same thing from you, what would be the point of having both of you in the group?"

What *was* the point of having me in the group? That, I still wasn't totally clear on.

"Stick with me," said Dee. "We'll figure you out. I'll focus on building your technique, if you'll concentrate on keeping it real, and remembering that an inexperienced honest performance will always be more effective than even an expert contrived one."

"Okay." That I could understand. Everything sounded so logical and attainable the way Dee put it. She was a Zen master of vocal technique. She did more than make me want to keep at it; she made me hope I might actually succeed.

I arrived at the studio calm and happy, ready to make the best of the new week.

"Hi, Julie!" I called out when I got in.

"Hey, Alya," she sang out, coming out from behind the pillar to administer the proper Montreal two-cheek-kiss greeting. That was a pleasant change.

Then Ange stepped into the room, from the washroom.

"Hi, Angelique," I said.

She walked quietly to the back of the room and sat down without looking at me.

Thus began the week of Angelique ignoring me completely—not the casual off-and-on ignoring of weeks past, but a studied, piercing ignoring—an ignoring too total to be ignored. It hung over every moment—interrupting the flow of every rehearsal, every conversation—loud in its silence, belligerent in its total avoidance of me. She looked out the window when I was singing. She brought in candy and shared it only with RJ and Julie. She brought up old inside jokes and complimented them on their clothes. And every time she dripped honey on them, it only seemed to highlight how not-spoken-to I was.

I refused to play along. The more she ignored me, the more I focused on our work. In rehearsals, I kept everything Dee told me in the forefront of my mind and concentrated on breathing right, keeping my tongue down in the back and my delivery as close to my speaking voice as possible. And I tried to find myself somewhere in the song, so I could communicate something genuine through my performance.

"Alya!" said RJ about halfway through the week. "You're already sounding way awesomer. You angling for a solo career this week? Ha haa."

"Thanks," I said, smiling, as Angelique slammed the change room door shut behind her.

Later that day, she finally rejected me formally on PopLife, and that's when I knew I was getting to her. To ignore someone that hard, you have to think about them all the time.

On Thursday, I decided to force a break to the silence. Normally, Angelique was the last one in the room for Raquo's sessions. But when I got back from lunch that day, she was already changed into her dance clothes, stretching aggressively by the window, pressing one leg up against the wall, forcing it over her head as hard as she could, her supporting leg trembling beneath her.

"You should be careful not to stretch too hard before you're warmed up," I said, walking by her to the change room. "You don't want to hurt yourself before—"

She leaned into the wall a little harder. "How do you know I'm not warmed up?" she snapped, then flinched, realizing she'd accidentally responded to me—a whole week of ignoring down the drain, just like that. By the time I had changed, she had given up on the contortions and was jogging in place.

I smiled and joined her, adding in jumping jacks. And as I did, something funny started to happen: Angelique started to copy me. At first I thought it was my imagination. I could see her only out of the corner of my eye. But I tested her, and she was definitely following me—trying to one-up me, even. I would jog; she would jog a little harder. I would do jumping jacks; she would do them twice as fast. A series of gentle shoulder stretches from me resulted in her twisting herself into back bends.

A mischievous idea started to form. I put on some music and started to do some top-rock—your basic introductory breakdance stuff, nothing crazy, just some classic steps, bouncing on the balls of my feet, boxing my shadow.

Sure enough, Angelique took it to the next level—aerobicizing to the beat, throwing in the hips of belly dancing and the feet of not just boxing but *kick*boxing.

Smiling to myself, I dropped to the floor and ran loosely through some foundation moves, letting my hands work their way around my feet. On the other side of the room, Angelique attempted what I think were supposed to be those kicks you see Ukrainian dancer guys do on PBS.

I did a little L-kick. She did a cartwheel.

Finally, I worked myself into a chair freeze and then tracked into a headstand.

Upside down, I watched her leap into the air, then land in the splits.

Only, I don't think it went quite the way she'd planned. As she fell to the floor, legs splayed, there was a long, slow ripping sound. And as I let myself down from my headstand, she twisted to see that she had ripped her white leggings from the inner thigh all the way up to the butt. And as if that weren't enough, as she stood up and bent over to investigate it further, another ripping sound echoed through the near-empty studio, only this time, it wasn't the tearing sound of cheap fabric that sang out from her butt, but the unmistakable trumpet of a single, long fart.

She froze for a second that felt like an eternity, scowled, and then bolted to the dressing room. I turned around, covering my mouth with both hands, trying not to laugh out loud. Raquo was standing in the doorway, smirking. He had seen the whole thing.

It was grim in the studio for the rest of that afternoon. Angelique was so rattled, she had an even harder time than usual following Raquo's instructions, and every time she missed something, he grew a little more impatient.

"It's walking, Hair. Walking! Left then right, left then right. Don't tell me you haven't done this before."

She nodded and took a deep breath, and then did it wrong all over again, falling on the wrong foot for the too-many-eth time in a row.

I don't think I would have been able to learn it with someone standing over me and yelling either. Raquo was no Dee. I decided, with disappointment, that although he was a brilliant choreographer, as a teacher, he was mean.

When I left the studio, Angelique was waiting for me outside. It was a hot night and the sun was just starting to set. Her hair was pulled back into a ponytail that fanned out behind her like a halo, catching the sun. In her tube top, heels, and tiny skirt, she looked, all farting aside, like a girl from a music video.

She is *a girl from a video,* I reminded myself with a pang of awe, forgetting for a minute that I would be one too. I shrank as I walked towards her. Her icy stare chilled the air by at least ten degrees. Maybe that's what accounted for the goosebumps that formed on my arms.

She opened her mouth to speak, and no sound came out. She tried again. "You win," she finally said, grimly.

"I win?"

"Don't act so innocent. I know you're smarter than that."

She thinks I'm smart! my brain registered, stupidly.

"I'll make you a deal," she said. "You help me with Raquo's stupid-ass choreography, and . . ."

I waited for the second part.

"Well, actually," she said, "I guess there is no 'and.' Just, you win. I need help."

"I don't need to win," I said.

"Bullshit," she said. "You can say that because you and Raquo have your own special little language, and you've got RJ thinking the sun shines out your butt."

"I do not!"

"Please. You just come in here like, *Oh, this is just*

something I do for fun on summer vacation. Like you're so much better than the rest of us."

"No—"

"Yeah. And you make smug little faces when I sing, and you laugh when I—"

"Angelique!" I said, just loudly enough to shut her up. "Stop. I'll help you."

Her face twisted into a sneer. "What?"

"I'll help you."

"And then what?" she said. "What do you want?"

"Nothing. That's it. I'll just help."

"Fine," she said. "Fine. I don't know what you're trying to pull here, but fine."

Seventeen

"What does any of this vampire crap have to do with the song?" Angelique asked after rehearsal the next day. We were alone in the studio. RJ and Julie had gone home already.

"Let's just forget the vampires for today," I told her. "Instead, try to think of something that would make you walk stiffly—like a hangover," I suggested, thinking of her PopLife profile.

"Have you ever even *been* hungover?" she asked, as if there was even one reason why *not* having had a hangover would be embarrassing.

I walked to the stereo, plugged in my iPod, and let one of Nadine's mixtapes play.

"That's not our song," said Angelique.

"I know," I said. "We're going to back it up a little before getting into the hard stuff. Besides, aren't you starting to get sick of 'Girl Fight'?"

"It's our *song,*" she said.

I stared at her.

"Okay, maybe a little," she mumbled.

"So," I said, starting to jog, "the first thing you have to do to not get your ass kicked by Raquo every day is be warmed up. So let's just jump around for a few minutes and find our groove—no steps, no rules, just pretend you're at home in your living room."

She looked at me suspiciously. "Can't we just focus on the vampire—I mean *stiff* thing?" she whined.

"No," I said. "You can't just never dance and then all of a sudden expect to be awesome at it because we're in rehearsal and you have to. Don't be embarrassed to let go. Being afraid of screwing up takes a lot of energy. Let's just shake it out before we try to move on."

"You are way too into this," she said, rolling her eyes. But she did it.

You can tell a lot about a person by how she dances. Like, Nadine's style is always aggressive, like the rest of her, and Madi is so precise about every little movement she can hardly relax, while Devin hams it up to cover for the fact that he might actually be brilliant if he could commit to anything.

Left to her own devices, Angelique danced like she was at a club—up on her toes like she was wearing heels, hips winding, arms in the air, hands drawing curves over her head, eyes closed as if she were bathing in the light of a disco ball. I felt almost like a voyeur. Whoever she was dancing for in that imaginary light, it wasn't me.

I cut the music, catching her mid-wind. She wobbled, then recovered quickly, striking a pose.

"Okay," I said, putting "Girl Fight" back on. "So now the actual steps. Why don't you start by showing me what you understand so far?"

She began to walk rhythmically across the room, emphasizing every other step, twisting her face into what I imagined was meant to be a vampire sneer—or maybe she just hated it *that much.*

"That's a good start," I told her. Something I learned from teaching kids is that people will almost always learn better if you tell them they're already doing awesome.

"No, it's not," she said. "It's *impossible.* It doesn't make sense. It's not even *walking.* I don't know what it is."

I smiled. The other thing I learned from kids is that one person in the room will always find a way not to believe you when you tell him he's doing awesome.

"That's just it," I said. "It isn't walking. It's more like being dragged against your will. You're not dancing the steps. Your body is dancing you."

"Great," she said dejectedly, but she positioned herself beside me in the mirror, ready to try again.

I went through it with her, tiny piece by tiny piece. Slowly, her negativity started to melt. The more she succeeded, the more she focused. Soon, an altogether different, triumphant Angelique started to emerge. I was seized again by that feeling of being drawn in that I had felt when I first met her. The "it" that RJ insisted I had—it oozed from her pores.

By nine-thirty, we were both exhausted.

"Raquo is going to lose his mind tomorrow when he sees how hard you've worked," I told her.

She finally smiled a real, genuine smile. Not a smirk, not a sneer, not a grimace or fake grin, but an actual smile—full, with teeth (they were perfect).

I felt proud then. I had cracked the code, found a secret button.

"I think this calls for a celebration," I told her.

"How are you enjoying the EnChantay experience so far?" said Angelique over the slab of chocolate–chocolate mousse cake we were sharing. "I mean, apart from me freaking out on you?" She looked down at the plate, almost sheepishly.

"Good," I said. "I think it's going to be really good. I mean, it's been a rush learning so much, meeting you guys, getting to work with a pro like Dee. I miss my friends but—"

"Do you have a boyfriend?" she asked.

"No."

She smiled. "I didn't think so."

"Why? Why do you say that?" I asked. Was she being mean again? Hinting that no one would want me? Or did she suspect—

"Oh, I don't know. You just seemed kind of . . ."

"What?" Oh god. She did suspect. I briefly considered jumping up from the table. But then she put her hand over mine.

"Don't be offended!" she said. "I just didn't think you did, that's all."

"So anyway," I squeaked, yanking my hand back, trying to steer the conversation to a safer place, "I think things are starting to go really good with the song. And Julie—"

"Omigod, I'm so tired of her telling me what to do all the time!" Angelique exclaimed. "Just because she's older. If I wanted to hear what my mom thought, I'd ask her. You feel me?"

And there we were, back in the deep end, swimming with sharks.

"Julie knows a lot," I said, shoving the largest bite of cake I could fit into my mouth, making it impossible to speak until I could think up a diplomatic response. "She can't help wanting to make everything perfect," I said, finally swallowing. "And she does so much extra work on the songs—"

Angelique waved it off. "She should have a solo career by now if she's that good. She's been in the industry *long* enough." She dipped the tines of her fork in the sauce without actually touching the cake.

Even as she let the poison drip from the tip of her tongue, she seemed so impulsive, so reckless, it came across as almost innocent. I was so secretly thrilled that she finally seemed to be opening up to me that I didn't consider the hollowness of her friendship with Julie, or how they would seem like best friends again in the studio the next morning.

The fork finally made its way to her lips. She let it linger there longer than was strictly necessary, and I fell a little further into the vortex of her Ange-ness.

"You know, Angelique," I said, attempting to change the topic again, "you could be a really good dancer if—" I was going to tell her *if* she listened more, *if* she practised more, *if* she cared about more than the steps. But I stopped myself just in time. "I think you're great."

"I am not," she said softly, looking down at her hands, fiddling with her fork again.

"Hey," I said, a mischievous impulse kicking in, "are you going to use that fork or just play with it?"

"What?" said Angelique, slightly frightened.

"It's good cake," I said, taking the fork from her and stabbing it into the last bite. I handed it back to her. She dodged it. "Oh, come on," I said, grinning, daring to taunt her with it. "Don't fear the mousse! It just wants to be loved."

She veered to her left just as I reached right. The mousse made contact with her cheek.

"Alya!" she shrieked. "I can't believe you did that!" Half the restaurant turned to see what the commotion was.

"I'm sorry," I said, starting to laugh.

"Do I have it on my face?" she said, diving into her bag to retrieve a mirror. "It's on my face, isn't it? I can feel it."

"No," I said, laughing harder. "Okay, yes, a little bit." It was huge. Half the mousse was on the fork and the other half was on her cheek. "But it's okay," I tried to persuade her. "You look good in it!"

She squinted pointedly at me.

"No, seriously, you could wear anything," I reconfirmed. "Someone should alert *Sizzle* magazine to the untapped cosmetic possibilities of mousse."

She took her finger, wiped the chocolate off her face, and slowly, exaggeratedly, licked it off. "Happy?" she asked.

"Yes," I said, glad I was sitting. My legs jittered under the table.

"This is fun," said Angelique.

"Yeah," I agreed.

"I'm really sorry we got off to a bad start," she said. "Can we try again?"

"Sure," I said. "Friends?"

She smiled. "Friends."

She reached her hand out to shake. I took it, and she pulled me into a hug. I felt like a giant as my arms circled her back. How, I wondered, could such a huge force be contained by such a tiny body? She was so light—almost breakable.

"Call me Ange from now on, okay?" she said.

"Sure, *Ange,*" Ange, Ange, Ange, Ange, Ange, I wanted to say, over and over again. It was a winning lottery number. Everything would be different from now on.

I was so excited, I called Madi from the cab on my way back to the dorm.

"Good news!" I told her. "Ange apologized for freaking out on me."

"Oh, it's 'Ange' now, is it?" she said.

"Yeah. I helped her out with some dancing stuff, and she chilled right out."

"That's . . . interesting," said Madi, using her journalist voice.

"How so?" I asked, defensively.

"She needed something from you, so she decided to be nice all of a sudden?"

"Not *exactly.* It's like I said. We're on the same team. We're *supposed* to help each other."

"Sounds manipulative," she said.

"Maybe *I* manipulated *her,*" I said.

"Okay, if you say so."

"I thought you'd be happy for me, Madi. You know how hard this has been."

"You're talking to me about someone I don't know, and who, from the sounds of it, I definitely don't trust. Someone has to watch your back, if you're not going to do it."

"Madi, what's wrong?" I said. "Why are you being like this?"

"Nothing," she said.

"Is it Trevor?"

"No!" she said. "Why do you automatically assume it's about a guy?"

"I don't— Wait a minute. Does that mean there *is* something wrong?"

"I told you. No."

"Madi—"

"Alya . . ."

"Fine. Maybe I shouldn't have called."

"Maybe you—"

"Bye," I said, and hung up, and then immediately wondered what had just happened.

Eighteen

"What are some songs you *cannot* sit still to?" I asked Madi that weekend. She seemed to be as desperate as I was to pretend our disastrous last conversation had never happened.

"I don't know . . . 'Holiday,' by Madonna, 'Blister in the Sun,' by the Violent Femmes, 'Tainted Love'?"

"Amazing," I said.

"Glad I could help," she said.

"No," I teased. "Amazing you can be a b-girl with such square taste in music. Do you know any songs from *after* 1995?"

"Amazing *you* can be a b-girl with such 'square' taste in vocabulary," she retaliated. "What's this for, anyway?"

"I'm making a mixtape for Angelique. And Julie. For both of them."

"Oh. My. God," she said.

"What?"

"I can't believe I didn't figure it out before. It all makes sense now!"

"What?"

"Last week you hated her, and this week you're making her mixtapes? You totally have a girl crush!"

"I'm sorry, what?" I snapped. "I was never hating on her. She was hating on me. And what the hell is a girl crush?"

What was going on? Why did it seem all of a sudden like every single person I talked to was trying to draw some kind of confession out of me?

"You know," Madi said. "When you look up to a girl and want to be friends with her, and you stay late to help her with stuff, and you start to ignore your other friends, and then you make her a mixtape?"

I huffed. "I do not do that! Besides, Ange is so not friend material. I *have* to work with her. I need to keep her on my side. I'm trying to be *professional.*"

"Okay, so no crush then. Whatever you say."

"Yo mama."

I made a mental note to stop talking about Angelique altogether. Things were getting too weird.

The final playlist for the mixtape was as follows: pop, electro pop, pop R&B, retro pop, pop hop, dance pop, and one old-school funk track for depth.

"Oh my god!" I imagined Ange saying. "You like Shiny Ray too? I *love* them! But what's Belgrave Wildlife Invasion? I don't think I've heard that." And it would become her favourite song, and she would always remember that I was the one who introduced her to it.

I took a Sharpie and wrote "Dare2Dance" across the CD face in bubble letters.

"What's this?" Ange asked when I handed it to her on Monday.

"Just a little mix I put together."

"Oh, thanks," she said, and tossed it in her bag without looking at it.

Suddenly I felt silly, standing there like a puppy, waiting for a reaction. It was a wake-up call. I was thinking about her when she wasn't around, but she could barely see me when I was standing right in front of her.

I chalked it up to bad timing. With our showcase happening that Wednesday, everyone was tense.

Julie had a sore throat. RJ suddenly wanted the last verse to be sung up a key "to ramp it up before saying goodbye." And then Ange, who had always sung "Girl Fight" so easily—almost lazily—started to crack under the mounting pressure, going flat in certain places and rushing in others. Once, she even blanked out on the lyrics for a whole verse.

"Have I not made it clear enough that this is make-or-break?" RJ shouted. "I have backers coming to this thing, industry people. This is no time to not be hot. We need them on our side, or there's not going to be an EnChantay, and you can all kiss your deals goodbye. Understand?"

Ange burst into tears, and from that point on, the more we practised, the worse it got. Eight times we ran through that song on Tuesday afternoon, and eight times Ange faltered on the high notes.

"It's okay," said Julie, over and over, as though the tension in her own voice wasn't obvious. "Just try again. You know you can do it."

But the more she sang, the worse it sounded.

"Take a break," suggested Julie. "Try a few deep breaths and focus on bringing the sound forward—"

"You're not my teacher," Ange snapped at her.

"We can't fight now," said Julie, sternly. "This is important."

"You think I don't know that?"

"Let's move on," said Julie. "We're running out of time."

"You move on. I'm done," said Ange. "I'm not going

to damage my voice for you." And with that she stormed out of the studio.

"Oh *mon dieu,*" said Julie, pressing her hand to her head. "Bad dress rehearsals always lead to great performances, right?"

"Yeah, totally," I agreed, without really believing.

Wednesday morning, RJ was in an inexplicably fantastic mood. Was he giddy because he knew something we didn't, or was it the insanity of certain failure that had brought a bounce to his step and a fidgety grin to his face? He kept tugging at the cuffs of his sleeves in a way that made me wonder what was about to fall out of them. I hoped it was more time.

At about half past ten, he burst out of his office and into the studio, stopping Angelique in the midst of what had been, up to that point, a series of interminable vocal warm-up exercises.

"*Mo-mo-mo-mo-mo, ma-ma-ma-ma, mo-mo—*"

"Enough of that!" he yelled. "You girls are in a rut. I don't want you obsessing over your mistakes all day. Change of plans: let's get out of here. Who likes surprises?"

"I do?" said Ange, wearily.

"RJ . . ." Julie warned.

I watched the three of them as if I didn't really have a say, because, let's face it, I basically didn't.

"No arguments!" he said. "We're getting out of here. I don't want you up on that stage tonight thinking about mistakes. I want you feeling like the stars that you are." He nodded with satisfaction, as if he'd been looking forward to using that line. "That's why," he said, "I have booked you all—"

Ange drew in a sharp breath of anticipation.

"A spa day!"

"Yeah!" shouted Ange.

Julie buried her face in her hands.

"Follow me," said RJ. "Your chariot awaits!" And with a grand arm flourish, he led us downstairs.

"Oh my god!" shrieked Ange as she reached the sidewalk.

Pulled up in front of the studio was a long, white limo—a stretch Hummer.

"This is going to be the best Wednesday of your lives," said RJ, beaming.

"RJ," said Julie, "this is . . . excessive. I mean, the fuel alone—"

"Aw, come on," said RJ. "Nothing's too sweet for my girls! Don't worry, Julie-Mom. It's not from the budget. It's a gift from Uncle J, your new favourite backer."

"Yeah, Mom, chill," said Ange, diving through the door RJ held open for us. Her head appeared through the sunroof a moment later. "Al, you gotta get in here and check this out!"

The car was purple inside—six different shades of it. From the shag carpet to the long curving seats, to the bar, the lava lamps—even the tinted skylights were purple.

"This is the *liiiife,*" said RJ, producing a bottle of pink champagne (which looked purple) from the ice bucket in the arm of his seat.

"Bet you never partied like this before," Ange said to me, reaching for a glass as she spread herself out like she owned the place.

RJ poured out three glasses of champagne, then handed me a raspberry ginger ale. "Everyone say, 'Thank you, Uncle J.'"

"Thank you, Uncle J!" we said, in tribute to the mysterious, absent backer.

"Don't worry, Alya, you can have a sip of mine when RJ's not looking," Ange whispered as she gulped back her champagne.

"Easy there, tiger," RJ warned her. "We need you conscious on stage, right?"

They laughed. Julie didn't.

"Aren't we starting the celebrations just a little early?" she said, but she was drowned out by our beat blasting over the stereo. I looked over to see Ange twisting the volume dial as loud as it would go.

The partymobile dropped us off at a day spa, where, again through RJ, Uncle J treated us to manicures and facials.

"This is the life," said Angelique, reclining in her chair with cucumber slices over her eyes, a masseuse rubbing her feet.

The star treatment didn't end there. No sooner had the polish set on our fabulous nails than we were escorted across town to the studio of Rachel—our new stylist!

Rachel's studio was on the seventh floor of a building in a trendy part of town. It was pretty basic, like our space, but with amazing huge windows and tons of sunlight. A huge chandelier hung from the centre of the room, over a waiting area with shabby-chic furniture upholstered in bright velvety fabric. One side of the room was nothing but racks upon racks of clothes. The other side had a basic office set-up and some sewing equipment. Piles of fashion magazines, bolts of fabric, and photos of models and musicians were everywhere. When we stepped into the room, Rachel was standing amidst all of this, saying goodbye to a group of girls who had to be models—all legs and neck and attitude—ignoring two ringing phones, a pencil wedged into her pink-and-teal ponytail and a measuring tape wrapped nonchalantly around her neck like it was a scarf.

"Wow, can you believe this place?" said Julie, running her hand over a bolt of black velvet.

"*Fantastique!*" said Ange, helping herself to a seat in the middle of the room.

"Be right with you, ladies, RJ," Rachel called over, as she escorted the models to the door.

"So tonight's the big night," she said a moment later, pulling the pencil from her hair and grabbing a clipboard off a nearby workbench as she crossed the room.

"You betcha," said RJ. "What hotness have you got in store for us?"

"I went through our sample racks and pulled some things I think might work," she said. "Which one of you is Angelique?"

Angelique mock-sheepishly lifted her hand. Girl had never had a shy moment in her entire life, but she sure could pretend when she thought it looked good.

Rachel sized her up. "Yes, yes, yes, good. Okay, so for you," she said, leading her by the elbow over to a rack of short dresses, all in bright jewel tones—reds, greens, purples, oranges, "I was thinking we'd go kind of flashy—big labels, top designers. That means that whatever you borrow off this rack, you'd better get it back to me in perfect condition, because these are all loaners. Understand?"

Angelique nodded enthusiastically. "Is this Versace?" she asked, fingering the hem of an orange strapless something or other.

"Yeah, why don't you hop over there and try it on for me? And be *careful!*"

It dawned on me that there was probably at least $20,000 worth of dresses on that rack alone. RJ wasn't kidding; we were getting the star treatment.

"Julie," Rachel said, wheeling out a second rack. "The idea with you is less flash, more taste. What we have here is all one-of-a-kind pieces from local designers. Whatever you go out in tonight, you can be sure it will never have seen the light of day—or of evening—before." She smiled at her own joke, and Julie gushed over the first thing her hand hit—a demure, black backless dress.

"Can I start with this one?"

"Be my guest," said Rachel.

I squeezed my hands together in anticipation, barely suppressing a squeal of excitement. I imagined myself taking the stage in gold or silver, with spaghetti straps and matching sandals, maybe the kind that tie halfway up your leg, and then dangling pendant earrings that would dust my shoulders under my upswept hair.

"Okay, Alya," said Rachel. "You're our active dancer—our young thing, not afraid to get a little sweaty out there."

I grinned. It was true. All true.

"For you, we're going sporty," she said, dragging a rack of what looked like cotton-spandex blends out from behind Julie's rack.

I must have looked stricken, because the next thing she said was "Don't panic."

Um, hello? Too late!

"Now, now," she said. "Everyone can't be the diva. Someone has to be our Left Eye or Sporty Spice, right? Balance! Contrast! And think of it this way: you'll stand out, in your own way."

I blinked.

"Oh, come now," she said, reaching into the rack. "It's not all bad. Here, try this." When she pulled her hand out, it was holding a pair of black satin booty shorts, with a bright blue halter top. Okay, fine. Not that bad. I smiled and took it from her, turning to go change.

"Oh, wait," she yelled after me. "Don't forget the socks!" And she tossed me a pair of red knee-highs. "They go with the PF Flyers." My eyes fell on a pair of red high-tops at the bottom of the rack. So much for sandals.

"Thanks," I said, laughing off my grimace, reminding myself that this was a *stylist* who was setting me up with *free clothes,* which I needed for my *recording career.* She could have dressed me in a spacesuit and I still should have been happy.

Despite having the most items to put on, I was the first one out of the change room. I studied myself in the mirror as Rachel poked and pulled at my outfit.

"It fits you perfectly!" she exclaimed. "How do you feel?"

"Okay." I shrugged. I guess I would have looked pretty hot in Rivercrest—overdressed even, no matter how incomprehensible the socks. And it *would* allow me to throw down at a moment's notice, which would have made Nadine happy back home. I smiled at that thought.

"You look pretty comfortable," said Rachel. "It takes a lot of confidence to pull off those shorts, but you seem to have it in spades."

"Thanks?" I said, unsure how much of an accomplishment it was to be able to wear shorts.

"Back to the change room with you," she said, clapping her hands together, satisfied. "You're done here."

RJ checked his watch as we left Rachel's den. "We're making good time, ladies, good time."

A vote was taken, and it was decided that we should break for a nap before dinner. Not that the day had been particularly strenuous, but RJ wanted us fresh on stage.

I felt ridiculously conspicuous when the massive limo dropped me off in front of the dorm, but not so ridiculous that I didn't lift my sunglasses as I looked around to see if anyone had noticed me getting out. (A couple of tourists had. I smiled at them graciously.)

Someday soon, I thought as I ate a cafeteria sandwich in my little grey room, we would release our record, and I would leave behind the sad dorm, the dingy studio, and the weekly train trips, and life would be all stylists and spas all the time—or if not all the time, then often enough to remind me why all the work was worth it. I fell asleep easily and dreamed of gold sequins and strappy sandals.

I woke up to my phone ringing.

"Get your sweet ass back down here and bring your appetite. It's T-minus-dinnertime!"

RJ had made reservations at a restaurant that was apparently "the hotness." It was so secret, you had to go in through the back door and walk through the kitchen to get to your table.

"Isn't this awesome? It's the only way in, so everyone feels like they're important enough to dodge paparazzi!" said RJ, pretending to take pictures with an imaginary camera. Ange vamped for him, almost elbowing a chef in the stomach as he sped across the floor with a steaming basket of something green.

As my eyes adjusted to the darkness of the dining room, a waiter guided me by the elbow to a seat in a booth at a small round table. Ange and Julie crowded in around me, with RJ sandwiched between them on the other side.

"Angelique," said RJ, "would you do us the honour of choosing a wine?"

She did, and when it arrived, it was pink again. She poured as we looked over our menus, and when I looked up again, my glass was full.

"I don't think so—" RJ started to say, reaching for it.

Ange put her hand out to stop him. "Oh, come on. It's just one glass with dinner. Lighten up."

He shook his head, but relaxed back into his seat.

I took a self-conscious sip. Ange raised her glass. "A toast! To EnChantay!"

"To EnChantay," we obliged.

She leaned her head back and drained her glass. I took a slightly bigger sip of mine.

"That's more like it," she said.

Julie raised an eyebrow, but said nothing.

Dinner had about a thousand courses, but each one was so tiny that what you mainly noticed was how long it took for it to arrive. By the time the meal was over, I was starving. Between each course, Angelique refreshed the wine, and I know she kept pouring for me because I caught her doing it once, when Julie was in the bathroom and RJ was texting under the table. She just put her fingers to her lips like "Shhh!" and kept pouring.

By the end of the meal, I was a little giddy and light-headed—but I couldn't tell if it was the wine or just nerves.

It was almost eight when we arrived at the salon to get dressed and made up.

"They stayed open late, just for you. Whaddya think of that?" said RJ.

We were whisked inside by a couple of harried-looking

stylists, who went straight to work spraying Ange's hair into a voluminous, feathery mass, twisting Julie's up into an elegant sculptural masterpiece, and mine . . . well, it was creative. They coiled each of my braids into pointy little cones and pinned them close to my head, so it almost looked like I had pointy short hair. *That's okay,* I thought to myself. *It'll make your makeup stand out more.*

But as the makeup artist approached me, her brush outstretched, RJ put a hand out.

"Nothing too glitzy, okay? We're running a low-key theme on this one."

This one? I set my teeth in a determined style as I saw a palette of bright, shimmering colours replaced with one of muted earth tones. I looked, in the end, like I wasn't even wearing makeup.

"I'm not a chick," said RJ, "but isn't that what the best makeup is supposed to look like? Ha haaa. Am I right? Is it hot? Do you love it?"

"Yeah, sure," I said, unable to suppress the last of my disappointment.

There was nothing left to do but get dressed and perform, and I found myself increasingly anxious to get it over with.

I carefully put on my outfit in the basement dressing room, then went back upstairs to wait for the others.

RJ appeared at the top of the stairs in a crimson velvet jacket with a gold dragon embroidered on the back.

"Not bad, eh?" he said. "What do you think?"

I held back a smirk, realizing that he had brought himself a special outfit when he wasn't even going on stage. "Very nice," I said. "Subtle. Are you wearing mascara?"

"Like it?" he said. "It's the hotness."

Julie appeared next, in a simple brown, sleeveless mini-dress, similar to the first one she had tried on, with a high collar and open back.

Then, after a considerable delay—just long enough for me to wonder why some people might not be comfortable in short shorts and start to feel strangely self-conscious in them myself—Angelique finally appeared at the top of the stairs.

I gasped. We all did. She wore a strapless lime-green satin number that made her eyes glow almost gold. But with a neckline scooping down to her navel and her skirt cut shorter than most of my shirts, there was no real risk that anyone else would notice her eyes. From the moment she appeared, the room dimmed and everyone around her—me, Julie, the stylists, even RJ, I think—blushed envy-green in the glow of the dress. I tried to avoid going blind as she presented herself on the top step, posing as though she expected someone to take a picture. It was like staring into the sun.

Ange produced a camera from her tiny satin purse and snapped a picture of herself before turning it on us. We smiled despite our inadequacy, and climbed back into the limo to the hoots and hollers of the salon staff.

Nineteen

The show was supposed to start at ten, but RJ kept us in the limo outside Club Gauche until ten-thirty.

"Make them wait," he said. "Let them wonder whose car this is. Make them hate you a little."

Julie sighed and rolled her eyes.

Finally, after a full fifteen minutes, there was a knock at the window. RJ slid it down, revealing the headset-clad, lizard-tattooed face of a bouncer. He opened the door for us and led us up an actual red carpet, past some velvet rope and a crush of people waiting to get in—girls who looked even younger than me, in heels and gold sequins; slick-haired muscle guys in too-crisp shirts; and the dejected kids who would just never be cool enough to even reach the carpet, with their gawky shoes and awkward hair—people who could have been Madi or Devin or me on any other night of the week. They either sneered or pouted or pretended not to notice as RJ shouted, "Make way for EnChantay!" parading us past them.

Ange stepped out of the limo last, posing for the crowd, demanding that they quake in the wake of the Dress. Julie kept her head down and followed me, close to RJ's elbows. A cigarette-smelling older guy with stubble leaned into me as we passed by. "See more of *you* soon," he said, grabbing my ass.

"Is he bothering you?" The bouncer—who apparently

had eyes in the back of his head—wheeled around and escorted the guy roughly back to a cab before the shiver had even made it all the way down my spine.

"See? I gotcha covered," said RJ.

Ange threw a protective arm around me, snapping a photo for posterity. I felt a jolt of excitement as I tripped after her into the club, and perhaps, I hoped, onto her PopLife page.

A DJ was spinning a down-tempo but loud hip-hop set as we entered the club and were escorted upstairs to a glassed-in VIP area that overlooked the stage. The club was bigger than I had expected—a lot bigger. It was like something you would see in a Mode TV segment on "Spring Break in Ibiza." The DJ stood to the left of the stage, where some band equipment was set up. Above him towered a huge projection screen, on which abstract images flashed in time to the beat. The crowd started to fill in as the bouncers slowly released people from the line outside, and my pulse quickened. I'd danced for big crowds before, but never sung, and this crowd was something else. They were beautiful people, dressed to the nines; they were used to being out. They'd probably seen a thousand shows, and they were expecting something big. They would eat us alive and then complain all over PopLife if we didn't deliver, I could tell. This was about more than just backers. This was our reputation on the line, before we'd even released a track. This was sink-or-swim time. I let it set in as the audience filed in like glittery, bronzed, demanding ants.

The first act didn't take the stage until almost 11:15—acrobats who worked the catwalk that projected into the audience as the DJ upped the intensity of the music. The blasé crowd half-watched, half-danced, half pretended to be more bored than they actually were, putting more effort into not spilling their drinks than to paying attention.

As they cleared the stage, RJ clapped his hands. "Ladies, there's someone I'd like you to meet."

I spun around to see a very small, older white guy in a grey suit standing meekly between RJ and an ice bucket full of champagne, smiling shyly and looking rather out of his element.

Okay, I thought to myself. *He doesn't seem too scary.*

"Uncle J, allow me to introduce Angelique Fielleux, Julie Cadet, and Alya Merchant."

"*Enchanté,*" said Uncle J, taking our hands one at a time.

RJ laughed. "Ha haaa—*enchanté,* EnChantay. Ha haaa—get it?"

Uncle J smiled awkwardly.

"I gotta tell ya, Uncle J, you are gonna be blown away tonight," RJ said to him in French.

"Fake it till you make it," RJ would explain later. "You gotta believe in it before you can make it real."

Down below, the music got louder. Uncle J told us good luck, and then retreated to join his other investment partners downstairs.

The next act was a b-boy crew that could have been the Hydra Force in some parallel dimension. I didn't get to see much of their set, because we were summoned backstage at that moment. It was then that it really began to dawn on me that I was actually going to have to get out there in front of that crowd and open my mouth and sing "Girl Fight" for real. Obviously we'd been working up to this all along, but it all seemed so disconnected and the day seemed so surreal, it was like I really didn't feel it until I was walking down the stairs and along the back hallway to the stage. Suddenly I was almost glad to be wearing sneakers. I don't know if I could have walked straight in heels, what with my legs slowly going numb with fear.

It's just one song, it's just one song, it's just one song, I repeated to myself over and over and over. *Four lines, four lines, four lines.* It almost worked, until I looked over at Julie and saw her face frozen in a wide-eyed grin of terror, mixed with concern, topped by dread. Ange had stopped smiling as soon as we'd reached the safety of the VIP area, which gave her an almost creepy aura of calm.

There was some cheering, the breakers left the stage, and then there was nowhere to hide. Our number was up.

"All right, all right," said RJ. "Let's do this!"

Julie smiled a last, tragic, desperate smile, looking almost like she might burst spontaneously into tears, or flames. I realized then how much worse it would be for her if we didn't do well. She was putting her existing career on the line, not just some distant, future reputation.

The MC announced our name and we walked stiffly to the stage together. I don't know whether it was all the practising or if RJ's day of bonding had actually done the trick, but for just that split second, I felt a genuine connection to them, like we were really a team. We glanced at one another, and then Angelique suddenly took my hand and Julie's and squeezed. "Let's kill this," she said, and I felt that we could.

When the lights finally hit us, we were standing proud behind our microphones. I was surprised to see a DJ and keyboardist on stage with us, because I had thought we would be performing to a taped version of our beat. I would later find out they were there for "authenticity," even though there were no records on the DJ's turntables and the keyboard was not actually plugged in.

As our beat burst over the sound system in huge stereo-surround quality, Angelique closed her eyes, listening for her cue, and I smiled at the surprise of hearing our music so large and all around us.

"So you got this man, and you think it's forever," Ange sang, right on time, right in key, pressing a hand to her left ear. *"Your love is real. Break it up? No way, never."*

"*No way, never*" came out the best I'd ever heard her do it. Angelique smiled big and powered through the rest of her verse.

"Don't you talk like that," Julie started in with a saucy twang I'd never heard before. *"Stop being foolish."*

Then Angelique kicked off the chorus—*"He's steppin' out wit'out you"*—gaining confidence with every line, until she was singing it so smugly, you'd have thought she was really enjoying it.

Finally it was my turn. Deep breath. *"Hey yo! Whoa, whoa, whoa, whoa! Don't go getting nasty."* I don't know whether it was because I was inspired by Ange and Julie, or if it was easy because I was expecting so little, but my voice came out steady and strong. Everything Dee had taught me, it's like I didn't have to think about it anymore. It was all there, cradled in my throat, behind my teeth, deep in my lungs, on the tip of my tongue. *"I know it hurts real bad, but let's keep it classy,"* I sang, and through my higher notes on *"classy,"* my voice unexpectedly opened up and shone through. It was like a clear, pure bell tone, totally controlled, in perfect harmony with the arrangement behind me. I saw RJ's face light up, and Uncle J, behind him, nodded in approval. All around them, the crowd nodded enthusiastically, and then I suddenly remembered: I loved being on stage. I loved it more than anything—the energy of the crowd, the rush of connecting with them, the pumped feeling that builds and builds every single second that you're getting it right. The tension left me, and my smile suddenly felt real. My knees were my own again; I risked a quick little spin and a step-ball-change-kick, and the people cheered for me, even though it was kind of weird with the lyrics.

"See? That's what she does, 'cause she can't face the truth," Ange countered, almost snarling.

"When you tell her like that, you come off soundin' rude," I reasoned, sweetly, batting my eyes exaggeratedly. RJ laughed.

"My guy is true to me. It's you I can't trust," Julie emoted, eyes cast down.

"Naw, she's got your back, girl," I asserted. *"Let's have a group hug."*

And just like that, my part was done. I relaxed and grooved along until the end, filling in parts of the harmony where I was supposed to, clapping along, letting the crazy rush of the night take over. Lifting my hands above my head, I got the crowd to clap along, and by the end of the song, everyone was on their feet, dancing, cheering, snapping photos with their phones. For the first time, I felt on top of my game, like I had a real place in EnChantay, and I understood what my purpose was.

"Amazing!" RJ shouted over the crowd as soon as the song ended. "Amazing!"

Uncle J met us backstage as L'Armée du Funk began their set-up.

"Was that amazing or what?" said RJ, slapping him on the back.

"Well," said Uncle J, nodding a bit to the beat as it faded out, "I am no expert, but very nice, very nice."

"Yes!" said RJ, jumping and pumping his fist in the air.

He ran a lap around the backstage area, which he finished by high-fiving each of us, including Uncle J. "Yes!" he said again. "You girls are the best! The best!"

"Thank god that's done!" Ange exclaimed loudly. "Now we party!"

RJ laughed. I yawned as all the built-up tension of the day finally left my body. A vision of my dorm bed came to me, and for the first time ever, it actually looked comfy.

"No, no, no!" said Ange, grabbing my hand and pulling me towards the dance floor. "I need you awake! We can't expect these old people to keep up with us!"

RJ laughed. "That's right. You guys are the show. I'm not the show. I don't have to keep up."

"The show?" I said. I thought we had just done the show.

RJ pointed to the dance floor, where the party was starting to heat up in anticipation of the headline act. "You're here to be seen, so go give them something to look at!" he said.

"You heard of EnChantay yet?" he asked random people as we pushed to the centre of the floor, handing them flyers as we went.

"What's *that?*" I yelled over the music, taking one from him. It was a glossy pink flyer, about the size of a CD case, with an image of three girls in silhouette, cropped from the chin to mid-thigh. Across their breasts in big gold letters was "EnChantay," with "Steppin' Out" across their hips.

"This is supposed to be us?" I asked, but he didn't hear me.

"Hot, yeah?" he shouted back over the music.

I handed it back to him, and he gave it to some guy in a silver shirt and white pants.

I gave up trying to be heard and shifted my focus to smiling and nodding enthusiastically no matter what was said to me. I hoped the bouncers still had my back like RJ said they did, but I soon realized it wasn't necessary. Ange and Julie had a subtle technique where the moment anyone got too close, one of them would somehow insinuate herself between us in such a way that the offending guy was blocked off. "Bermuda Triangle in effect," said Ange.

L'Armée du Funk took to the stage, and that's when the party really got going. They had obviously built an enthusiastic following, and the louder and faster the music got, the harder we danced, the sweatier the crowd grew. As their set wound down and a new DJ took over, the music only got more intense, the lights more spinning, the crowd more drunk. It was around then that Julie begged off, and RJ followed not long after.

"So soon?" Ange pouted.

"Soon?" he yelled. "It's after two!" He gestured at me. "She's with you now, understand?"

"Oh, don't worry. I'll take care of her," said Ange, winking at me.

"Take it easy tomorrow," he yelled as he left. "Come in at noon!"

No sooner had RJ left than Ange spun around and produced, from the solitary fold of her dress, an Amex card. "Look what I have!" she yelled.

I squinted at it. It was RJ's.

"Where'd you get that?"

"Come!" she said, hooking her arm through mine. "We've only got an hour. Let's make the most of it."

She dragged me up to the bar, where we stood waiting for the bartender. It was nice to get a bit of air—I hadn't realized how hot it was on the dance floor until I stepped away from it.

The card went over the bar and back across it came a row of tiny drinks in shot glasses, each one darker and more mysterious than the last. Ange held up a glass, brought it to her mouth, and downed it in one gulp.

"What are you waiting for?" she asked, watching me examine mine like it was a science experiment.

Okay, I thought, *here goes.* I brought it to my lips and let it slide back in one shot. The sweet, sticky liquid stung my throat, twelve flavours at once—cinnamon, cloves, cola, licorice, bubblegum, and fire. I tried not to cough as it hit my throat.

"Whoo!" said Ange, picking up a second glass, and I found my hand mirroring hers. We locked eyes, tilted our heads back, tossed care to the wind and good after bad, and swallowed.

Shots two and three went down like pure maple syrup and nail polish remover. I don't remember the fourth one, but I'm pretty sure it was blue.

Ange giggled and grabbed my hand. We ran back to the dance floor.

By now, the bass was so loud and heavy I could feel it climbing my legs through the floor, pushing me to move, move, move.

"This is on that CD you gave me!" Ange yelled, leaning into my ear, still dancing.

"You listened to it!" I yelled back

"It was awesome! You are awesome!"

She threw her arms around me in the most awkward, spectacular, messy, fantastic hug. I stumbled backwards, and she fell into me. I grabbed her tighter, recovered my footing somehow, despite the growing numbness in my legs, and got us both back to standing without falling over.

All around us, the room seemed to move faster and faster, and the faster it went, the faster I wanted to go. I spun and spun until some chick whacked me accidentally on purpose with her handbag, and I noticed her boyfriend staring at me. Ange pulled me into her again.

"Everyone is watching us!" she said, beaming.

"They are?" I said, stupidly.

"Let's give them a real show!" Before I could figure out what she meant, she grabbed me by the waist and began to grind her body against mine in time to the music.

I laughed, barely able to control my legs, let alone the rest of me, and I let my arms loop around her shoulders. We wound together, eyes locked, the crowd closer, my ears falling deaf to the hooting and hollering of all the guys cheering us on. All that mattered was the closeness between us, the sweet smell of her hair, the sweat on her neck, the feeling of the room disappearing around us and—

"We're having fun, right?" Ange asked.

Or was it "We're *just* having fun"? The more I replay this, the less I remember. I'm afraid that one day soon, I'll have lost it all.

I nodded. She reached up with her right hand and drew me closer until our lips were touching. I hesitated, surprised at first, but as she pressed into me more insistently, I let myself kiss her back. *She* is kissing *me,* I told myself. *She* started this. Ange did. The thought was more intoxicating than all of the shots put together, or the tangy citrus taste of her tongue and the salt of her skin. I melted into her, turned into a puddle. I held her close, eyes closed, slippery hands clumsily grabbing at sweaty limbs. And then, from some far-off, never-before-heard-from, inebriated corner of my brain, a single, clear thought rang out: *This is what it's supposed to feel like.* It was exactly like I'd never had the guts to imagine it.

Ange separated herself from me, laughing.

More, I thought, my eyes closing to block out the too-harsh lights that pulsed above us. *More of that, right now.*

When I opened my eyes next, I was on the floor.

"Ange!" I said with alarm, and then I saw her leaning over me, fanning me with my purse. A couple of bouncers helped me to my feet and handed me back over to her. She struggled to help me walk to the door. All I cared about was that she was holding my hand.

"I just need some air," I said. "I'll be okay when I get some air."

"You'd better be," she growled.

We grabbed our jackets, and I followed her awkwardly out into the night. The limo was gone. The driver had probably gone off duty hours before. The air was cold. I shivered as Ange called us a cab.

"Where are we going?" I asked sleepily as the cab navigated through unfamiliar streets.

"I can't send you back to the dorm like this. You're past curfew anyway. I guess you're coming home with me."

"Mmmm," I said, and then I'm pretty sure I nodded off in the back of the cab, with my head in her lap.

I was jostled back to consciousness by Ange shaking me in the cab.

"Come on," she said. "I can't carry you."

We hobbled together up her spindly spiral staircase. She clumsily let us into her apartment, and we shushed each other all the way down the hall, her heels awkwardly clapping against the hardwood floor.

"Quiet," she whispered. "My roommates are sleeping."

"*Trying* to sleep!" called a roommate, and I started to giggle.

Angelique grabbed me by the wrist and yanked me into her room. I stumbled through the door onto her bed, losing a shoe along the way, which only made me laugh harder. Ange climbed on top of me and put a hand over my mouth to shut me up. When that didn't work, she kissed me again.

I wrapped my arms around her, drowned in her hair, let her bed swallow me whole.

This is what it's supposed to feel like, I thought to myself again. *This must be it.*

Twenty

This must be alcohol poisoning, might have been more like it.

I woke up surrounded by soft white sheets, with the sun streaming in all around me. A crystal in the window cast coloured shards of light on the exposed brick wall at the head of the bed.

I sat up quickly and immediately regretted it. Shooting pain attacked my brain from every direction. I flopped back down against the pillow. That was better. I closed my eyes and felt a cool breeze waft in through the window, and started to drift back to sleep, slowly remembering the night before—dancing with Ange, her lips. Had that really happened? It felt so far away.

My ears were ringing. I pressed on them to make it stop, but I couldn't turn it off, no matter how I tried.

Ange's room was big and cool. There were piles of clothes strewn about every surface. She had photos of herself at various ages stuck up around the mirror of her dressing table—there was Ange at a tap recital, Ange winning a beauty pageant, Ange in skates, Ange at Christmas, Ange at the prom. There were school photos from three different schools. It looked like she must have moved around a lot. In several of the photos she was wearing ribbons or holding trophies. She was a winner.

Lying there, half-awake, surrounded by her things, I realized how little I actually knew about her, and then, with a shock of excitement, how much more I wanted to get to know. I closed my eyes again and tried to replay her kiss in my imagination.

Then it hit me: bright sun? What time was it?

I found my bag beside the bed and reached for my phone. It was dead. Crap. Crap, crap, crap, crap, crap.

"Ange?" I called, scrambling out of bed. I was in my underwear. My tiny shorts were crumpled at my feet. I got a whiff of myself and just about passed out. Had I smelled that bad the night before? Oh god.

"Ange?" I called again, opening the bedroom door a crack to peer down the hall.

An unfamiliar woman looked up from a computer in the living room. "She left already. You should too."

I slowly became aware of a nasty, creeping feeling all over my skin, like I hadn't washed in a month.

"Shower?" I asked pathetically.

"On your right. Take a towel from the cupboard. Don't make a mess."

"Thanks," I said, embarrassed. "Um, I'm Alya, by the way."

"Yeah," she said. "I know."

I had, at this point, some idea how much shit I was going to be in when I finally showed up at rehearsal, but it was catching a glimpse of myself in the bathroom mirror that really brought it home. My hair was fuzzy on one side and matted on the other. My eyeliner had run and my mascara had blurred, giving me dark, hollow raccoon eyes. My teeth and tongue were blue from whatever it was I had swallowed last, and I had an oblong bruise on one cheek (I guess from how I fell?) that threatened to spread into a black eye.

I climbed into the shower, hoping for a miracle. I washed my hair with shampoo I found on the edge of the tub, wishing there'd been an Undo button under it. As I towelled off, my thoughts turned to bargaining. *Take me back in time,* I prayed, *just far enough to get to the studio by noon, and I will never stay up late again.*

Maybe it would be okay. Maybe Ange had talked to RJ. But why hadn't she woken me up before she left?

I wrapped myself in my towel and hurried back to Ange's room to get dressed. That's when I realized I only had my tiny evening bag with me. My big bag with my clothes had stayed in the limo when I went into the club.

I gingerly climbed back into my show clothes and called a cab. I would have to go back to the dorm to change. There was no way I was showing up at rehearsal wearing what was quickly becoming the Outfit of Shame.

"Two-thirty!"

That's what time it was when I got to the studio, bruise, dark glasses, and all.

"Two-thirty!" RJ kept shouting. "Not hot, Alya. Not even cool."

There were extra people in the studio—our stylist, Rachel, and a grey-haired man with dark-rimmed glasses. They were bustling about, debating with RJ and taking measurements. A white screen was set up against one wall. Powerful lights were aimed at it. It looked important.

"What's going on?" I asked with dread.

"Just a little something called screen tests and costume fittings. Do you have any idea how expensive this is? Do you know how much of Uncle J's money you're wasting?"

"I'm so sorry. I didn't know this was—"

"It's not your job to know. It's your job to show up on time! Two-thirty!"

"I know," I said. "But it's never happened before and it won't happen again, I promise."

"You wouldn't even answer your phone. Where the hell have you been?"

"I was—" I struggled to give him some kind of explanation. It would have helped if I'd had some idea of what had happened myself. All I knew was that one minute I was falling for Ange, and the next I was leaning on her because I couldn't feel my feet. It seemed prudent, somehow, not to tell him. And, perhaps stupidly, I didn't want to drag her down with me.

"I overdid it last night, and then I overslept this morning. My phone died. It won't happen again."

"No, it won't," said RJ. "Until you figure out how to be professional, your partying days are over. If you're going to act like a kid, we're going to treat you like one."

"Is Ange—?" I started to ask.

"Angelique is your bandmate, not your babysitter," he said. "Remember that."

My head started to spin again.

"Now," said RJ, "I won't mention this to your parents if you don't, but this can never happen again. Do we have a deal?"

It hadn't even occurred to me to tell them. My parents were the last thing on my mind.

"Do we have a deal?" he asked again, nervously.

"Yeah. Thanks," I said, confused.

I needed to talk to Ange. I needed to find out what had happened, what she was thinking, when we could be alone again. But the day was too busy. As soon as I was done talking to RJ, I had to go get a thousand measurements taken by Rachel. I replayed the night before in my head as she took notes about everything from my wrists to my inseam and ankles. I absent-mindedly answered her questions, thinking only of the mischievous glint in Ange's eyes, the lurch of my stomach when she appeared in the Dress, the row of shots on the bar. My ears continued to ring all day, making it feel like I was trapped behind a glass wall. I could see people's lips moving, but the sounds that came out were oddly quiet and far away. I got marched over to a screen test where, behind my wall, I experienced, over and over again in slow motion, the sensation of Ange's hand on the back of my neck, pulling me closer. Had it even happened the way I remembered it? There were so many holes.

"Alya!" snapped David, the director. "We're rushed enough without you ignoring my instructions."

I tried to focus as he instructed me to stand this way, turn my head, sing my lines. I tried to turn my bruised cheek away from the camera, but he wouldn't let me. All the while, my head pounded harder and harder. The lights threatened to burn holes in my retinas.

And every time I looked across the room at Ange, she was looking somewhere else.

I finally caught her alone in the change room at the end of the day.

"What did you do to me last night?" I joked. "Those drinks were so small—"

"Your hand brought them to your mouth," she said, staring into the mirror, where she was touching up her lip gloss. Maybe I imagined her frosty tone. My head hurt so much, I couldn't tell which way was up.

"Just kidding," I said, smiling nervously. "What are you up to after this?"

"I have plans," she said, picking up her bag, training her eyes on the floor.

"Oh, too bad," I said. "Maybe I'll call you later?"

"I guess," she said.

"I don't have your number," I said, reaching into my bag for a pen.

She put her hand out to stop me.

"Alya," she said, "I think it's better if we don't hang out anymore."

My chest clamped up. Panic. Confusion.

"I know you won't understand," she said, "but this is everything to me. You're this amazing dancer, and Julie can do, like, *everything.* She even plays *instruments.* This is it for me. I don't have a choice. I can't do anything that's going to mess up my big break."

"We could just be friends," I told her. "We can be anything you want."

"I'm sorry," she said. "I didn't come here to make friends."

And then she left.

The door slammed shut like a punch to my other cheek. I sat down on the bench and hung my face in my hands to quiet the pounding in my head, swallowing hard against the sob that threatened to well up in my throat.

I felt so—embarrassed? Betrayed? Stupid? Words were so inadequate. They could hint around the edges, but nothing could come close to naming the overwhelming, raw surge of horribleness that reared up and tried to strangle me from the inside. I felt like the walls were closing in on me. I felt like swallowing myself whole. I had to get out of there. I grabbed my bag and crashed through the door, not realizing Julie was on the other side, about to come in.

"Alya!" she said as she recovered her balance. "Are you okay?"

"Fine," I squeaked.

Her eyes narrowed in on my bruise. "Are you sure?"

"Yes."

And then, as fast as I could, I darted to the stairs and out to the street.

Twenty-one

I didn't know where I was going when I left the studio. I just knew I couldn't go back to the cold, lonely, empty dorm—I couldn't be by myself. So I walked for an hour or more, and for the better part of that hour, I threw myself into denial.

Knowing Ange, she could change her mind. Everything could be different the next time I saw her. She was like that—angry one minute, forgiving the next. Maybe she just needed time to think. Maybe she would be waiting for me outside the studio again in the morning. *Let's take it slow,* she would say, and then I'd nod and give her a hug, and tell her I understood.

In this fantasy, we ended up making out again, and I almost walked into a lamppost.

I imagined telling Raniya and Gina about Ange.

"Right on. Way to go," imaginary Raniya would say about the makeout incident.

"Forget the bitch," imaginary Gina would chime in.

Then imaginary Raniya would say, "What the eff are you doing in a group with these people anyway? They sound repressed."

"Yeah, lose 'em," imaginary Gina would say. "I'm thinking of starting up this lo-fi band. You should join."

"I know! Let's have a coming-out party! There's this chick from Toronto you should totally meet."

That's not what I wanted. I wanted to call Madi and have her tell me that everything would work out—that Ange would definitely change her mind, that I hadn't imagined something between us. And I wanted to believe that Madi herself wouldn't be freaked out by just the idea of me with another girl.

But the way things had been between us lately, I couldn't predict what she would say. I realized there was only one person on Earth I could talk to.

I landed on Dee's doorstep half an hour later, and fidgeted for at least five minutes before working up the nerve to ring the bell. I should have called first—from a pay phone, at least. I was going to be interrupting, I knew. She would be pissed or confused. She wouldn't even be home.

She answered before the chimes were done chiming.

"Alya!" She stepped back at first, looked me up and down. I lifted my sunglasses; no point hiding the bruise. "Honey," she said.

"I'm sorry," I said, shaking my head—for barging in on her unannounced, for not living up to what she thought I was, to what *I* thought I was, too.

"No," she said, stepping forward and wrapping me in a hug. "If you're here, I know it's important. Don't ever be afraid to come to me."

With her arm around my shoulders, she guided me inside.

"It's late. You must be hungry."

I wasn't hungry. I was too freaked out to be hungry. But I nodded anyway because it felt like the right thing to do. I probably would have nodded no matter what she said. *I'm just about to go into space in this homemade shuttle.* Okay. *Let's go out in the backyard and howl at the moon.* Okay. Not knowing what else to do, I turned myself over to her entirely.

She put on the kettle, made me a sandwich, and didn't press me for explanations.

"Are you tired?" she asked. "Do you want to lie down?"

Tears started to well up in my eyes. She was too good—far, far too good. I'd got myself into this mess and—

"Come, I'll put you up in the guest bedroom."

I followed her upstairs, and she led me past the studio to a small, cool room at the back of the house with just a twin bed and a round table with a lamp on it. She turned back the covers, and I climbed in, noticing how soft the sheets were. Then, like it was the most natural thing in the world, she tucked me in. "Sleep well," she said, pressing a hand to my cheek. I nodded one last time, closed my eyes, and miraculously, slept.

I woke up a couple of hours later to the sound of piano music drifting softly from down the hall. I sat up, put my feet on the floor, and felt the firmness of the mattress under me. Yawning, I stretched and stood. I felt wobbly. I shook it off, and quietly opened the door and padded down the hall, stopping just outside the music room. Through the half-open door, I could see Dee seated at the piano. She played softly, her eyes closed, head back, fingers moving over the keys as if she was pouring the sound into them and they might have been silent for anyone else.

I didn't recognize the piece—it was bluesy, smooth, intricate, warm. She opened her mouth and began to sing—a simple song with a repeating chorus, almost like a meditation.

I brace myself,
Gripping my heart in my clenched fist,
But it cannot be contained.
Love. Open eyes, drink it in,

Let it go, watch it fall away.
My breath will carry me home.

It was so different from anything I'd heard before. Quiet but large, intimate but open, controlled but free. It was like everything Dee had been trying to instill in me come to life. It was soothing, like a mantra. *My breath will carry me, my breath will carry me, my breath will carry me.*

I stepped forward into the room. Dee opened her eyes and smiled, seeing me for the first time, but kept playing. Hesitantly, I added my small voice to her all-encompassing one. I harmonized in my own way, as I felt out the melody, not caring if the sound came out raspy or if I missed a note here and there. Music filled my chest, moved through me, overwhelmed me, and for a moment I understood fully what Dee had been trying to teach—honesty, openness, letting myself out, basking unashamedly in my own inexperience, hiding nothing.

When the song ended, I sat down by the piano and told Dee the whole story, starting and ending with Ange.

Dee listened without interrupting. When I was done, she stepped back and looked at me thoughtfully. Finally, she said, "There's someone I think you should meet."

Dee persuaded RJ to give me Friday off. I overheard her talking to him on the phone the next morning. She sounded angry.

"No, RJ," I heard her say. "You have a responsibility to these girls and— She is *sixteen* and away from home— No, you listen to me! Either you do or I'm going to have to stop working with you. You know I don't make idle threats."

After she hung up she came and found me in the music room, where I was awkwardly poking at keys on the piano.

"RJ will be by later with the rest of your things. You'll be staying with me from now on. I hope that will be acceptable to your parents. I'll talk to them for you."

I nodded, wide-eyed.

"You don't have to worry. RJ understands how things need to be," she said ominously. "Now, do you have something nice you can wear to lunch, once your luggage gets here?"

I nodded again, still too amazed and bewildered and grateful to say anything.

An hour later, my luggage did arrive. I dressed as neatly as I could in the travelling outfit my mother had bought me at the beginning of the summer. It didn't feel as glam as it had that first week. The shorts had shrunk enough in the wash that they pulled at the waist. The jacket was too heavy for the season. The sandals were tacky. It just felt like a costume for another Alya, a dress-up Alya—Confused Starlet Alya, Identity Sold Separately. *Oh well,* I thought, as I criticized myself in the mirror. It had one thing going for it: it was honest. It was probably the last time I would wear it.

At lunchtime, we drove in Dee's impossibly elegant cream-coloured car to a small but chi-chi bistro not far from her place. Bracing myself against the creamy tan armrest, I marvelled all the way there at how much style she had, gliding around traffic at a maniacal speed, perfectly relaxed, not a hair out of place.

She wouldn't tell me who we were meeting. "You'll see," was all she'd say.

I craned my neck as I followed her into the restaurant. "Dee," I said nervously, "I am totally under-dressed!"

"You're fine," she said.

Thank goodness my bruise had faded enough to be concealed by makeup.

Dee spotted someone across the room. "Oh good, he's here already!" She raised her hand and waved. A slight, youngish black guy waved back, but I couldn't get a good look at him over Dee's shoulder.

As we got closer, the dude stood. He was a little shorter than me, wearing a basic khaki shirt and crisp dark jeans, again making me feel totally shlumpy by comparison. He held out his arms to hug Dee and smiled, and that's when I realized:

Oh. My. God. It was Bershawn!

He looked so much smaller in person—young, somewhat timid.

"Alya," said Dee, "this is—"

"Bershawn!" I interrupted. "You're Bershawn Sera!"

"Thank you for noticing," he said, with a shy smile.

"I love you!" I blurted.

"Thanks." He laughed gently.

"I have all your CDs! My friends and I tried to go your concert!"

He smiled again.

"I'm not going to do this for the whole meal, I promise!" I said and buried my embarrassed face in a menu. It was so weird to be sitting across the table from him, like he was some guy—some normal, regular guy—and not *Bershawn*. I tried not to stare.

The waiter came to take our orders. I can't remember what I ate that day, but I'll remember forever that Bershawn ordered an avocado salad and a lime Perrier.

"So," he said, "you're down with EnChantay, right? How's that going?"

I almost spat out my water. "You've heard of us?"

"I haven't heard much about the group, other than what Dee has told me," he said. "But that lead singer—what's her name? Anastasia something?"

"Angelique," I finished quietly, without even bothering to point out that we were an ensemble and therefore had no lead singer.

"*Everybody* is talking about her. More about her partying than her singing, though," he said. "You hang out with her?"

"We're going into the studio next week," I said, pretending I hadn't heard him. He exchanged a quick glance with Dee across the table.

"Oh, yeah?" he said. "They doing the old Cap thing? Releasing the video before the album's even in the can?"

"Yeah, I guess," I said.

"Who've they got doing choreo?"

"Raquo."

"Oh, yeah?" he said. "I love R. He's crazy. What's he got you doing? Skydiving or something?" He grinned widely. "I hope you take the time to enjoy it. I remember how it was when I was just starting out," he said. "There was so much going on, everything happening so fast, I hardly had a minute to stop and think about what I was doing."

"It wasn't all enjoyable," Dee interjected.

"It was a blur," he continued. "One minute I was this average, mostly-Bs high school student. Next, I was on a tour bus in I-don't-know-where USA, Japan, Europe, you name it. I had to quit school and bring a tutor on the road with me. It got so bad, I'd be memorizing stuff for a geography exam when I didn't even know what country I was in."

I smiled uncomfortably. "I have to go back to school in September," I said. "That's why we're recording everything now."

"If the single's hot, they're going to make you drop out," he said matter-of-factly.

Worry started to rise in my throat. My parents were *never* going to let me drop out of Rosewood. Not even for a tutor. I wasn't even sure *I* would want me doing that.

"For the first few years," Bershawn continued, "all I could do was go where I was told, do what they said—I even dated who they said I should date."

"Felishia?" I asked, remembering the "love of his life," the big breakup, the subject of his entire second album.

"Yeah," he said, hanging his head. "That was all for the photos."

"Whoa." I leaned on the table for stability while I took that in. I'd been in the seventh grade when that scandal hit. All my friends were so happy he had broken it off with her, because it meant he might maybe someday, somehow wind up with them. I was kind of bummed. Felishia was cool. They did good duets together.

"Hey, don't look so sad," he said. "It's just business."

I grimaced into my salad. Luckily, at that point Dee cut in and the conversation went in a whole other direction—people they knew and I didn't, how they were doing, who was sick, who'd just had a baby, whose comeback album was going to tank. I didn't mind. I felt like I'd already heard too much.

"Alya, it was so nice to meet you," said Bershawn at the end of the meal. And then, when we all got up to leave, he hugged me. *Bershawn* hugged *me!*

"There's my ride!" he said as a small black convertible pulled up in front of the restaurant. "I'll come by again before I have to go back to Toronto," he called to Dee as he jogged across the street. "I promise!"

What happened next unfolded in slow motion, or at least that's how I have to replay it in my mind to make sure I wasn't making any of it up. A blond guy got out of the car. Bershawn gave him a buddy handshake, then leaned in for the traditional two-cheek Montreal kiss, only the other guy pulled him in further for a hug, then kissed him full on the lips. It wasn't a mistake. He meant to do it. And Bershawn kissed him back before backing away and looking over his shoulder, as if to check whether anyone had noticed.

My jaw dropped involuntarily. He saw me and hesitated, then looked at Dee from across the street like, *I thought you said she was cool. Are we going to have a problem here?* If Dee noticed, she didn't react. I finally managed to return my jaw to its normal position and waved goodbye. He waved back uncomfortably, then the blond guy walked around to the passenger side of the car and got in, tossing Bershawn the keys. Bershawn climbed into the driver's seat and they drove away.

"Bershawn is gay!" I blurted to Dee as I got into her car.

"I guess you could say that," she said, casually throwing the car into gear.

"But his songs—they're all about girls! Felishia, Alicia, Maria, baby girl—I thought—"

She shook her head.

"He's had a rough time. He only started to come out just as his career was taking off. His parents disowned him. What could he do when his producers sat him down to tell him they didn't think their customers were ready to support his lifestyle?"

"No!" I cried. "His real fans would support him no matter what!"

"Maybe, but not enough to make him a star."

"But isn't it hard? Doesn't it hurt to have to watch himself all the time?"

"Don't worry about Bershawn, Alya. Business is business. He has a good life. What will you make of *your* life? That's the real question."

Its just business, it's just business, it's just business. The now-familiar refrain ran through my mind on repeat, and a single question rose above it: If business was just business, music was just business, and life was just business, what was left? Why did anyone bother doing business in the first place?

Back home that weekend, I sat on the edge of my bed and let the truth sink in.

Bershawn was gay.

So was I.

I tried that on a couple of times. I, Alya Merchant, liked girls.

I declared it out loud to my mirror:

"I am a lesbian."

I was surprised to find it felt pretty good.

"I am a lesbian," I said again, and I felt a tingle of excitement—stronger than when I'd opened my Rosewood acceptance letter but slightly less intense than when I was dancing on stage.

"I am a lesbian!" I said at full voice, not even caring who heard me anymore.

Devin knocked on my door. "What are you yelling in there?" he demanded.

"Nothing!" I shouted back.

Okay, I *almost* didn't care. It was a start.

Twenty-two

On Monday morning, it was like Ange and I were meeting for the first time.

"Good morning, Ange," said Julie when she came in.

"Morning, Ange," I parroted glumly.

"Ange*lique,* please," she corrected.

I curled my fingers into tight fists and fought to keep my smile.

It was presentation day. RJ was sitting behind a table with Rachel and David and a buff new woman who looked like a fitness instructor. What had the stylists decided? I wondered. That we needed pumping up to make us hotter? I was sure the explanation was bound to have the word "hot" in it, whatever it was.

"Good morning, everyone!" RJ said, adjusting the sleeve of his suit, which was an uncharacteristically quiet charcoal affair, so sensible it might have been stolen from Uncle J's closet. "I want to start," he said, "by saying how totally, perfectly *awesome* everything's been going. You three have been doing *uh-mazing* work, and I couldn't be any happier with it. The song, your moves, everything—it's all been exactly on point, just precisely the way we want it. It's hot, and we love it.

"All that's left is for Rachel and David to take your perfection, make it that much perfecter, and immortalize it for all time and forever on video. But like I said, you guys are fantastic, so we're hardly going to have to change anything at all. Do you agree, David?"

"Yes," said David. "It's rare that we get a group that's already the total package, but with EnChantay—and I think Rachel will agree with me here—it's like the hard work has already been done for us. I almost feel like I'm cheating. At the end of the day, this is just a game of playing up strengths, which are many, and minimizing a very few petty weaknesses so they aren't distracting."

Rachel giggled in agreement. "But we don't want to send you out there naked, right? So we're just going to do a little tweaking and polishing, so when people see you in that video or you take to the stage, it's pure magic."

"Are you ready to see what they've come up with?" said RJ.

"Yeah!" cheered Angelique and Julie. I feigned enthusiasm.

"Okay," said stylist Rachel, moving a streak of teal-and-pink hair out of her eyes. "Let's start with Angelique, our diva: petite figure, great hair, reads brilliantly on camera. What we're going to do with you is go big."

She threw an artist's sketch of Angelique up on the screen. The stick figure in the drawing wore a bra and tiny skirt under a bright pink overcoat with matching boots. Stars were coming out of her hair.

"As you can see," continued the designer, "we've got bright colours, shiny finishes, huge makeup, gigantic cleavage, tons of skin, hair for years, high boots with skyscraper heels—everything is just big, big, big."

Angelique nodded approvingly. Everyone clapped.

"Next up, we have Julie. Now, it's important to keep in mind here that while EnChantay is a group, we're trying to craft three distinct personalities for our girls. We want to send a message that each of you is unique and different, and that's why you work so well as a team—because it's the music you have in common. So, for contrast, with Julie we're going to go for a more sober, serious, dare I say *mature* look."

Julie winced at "mature" as Rachel threw up a sketch of a tall woman in a funny kind of tuxedo, where the pants were slit on each side all the way up to the hip. She was wearing strappy heels with spats, a bustier under the jacket, a bow tie, and a tall, sequined hat.

"It's businesslike, but it's a sexy kind of business. Exotic," said Rachel. "And I believe, David, you had something you wanted to add here?"

David cleared his throat.

"Yes, in keeping with this dark mystique we want to give you, we're going to change the spelling of your name."

"I'm sorry?" said Julie.

David advanced the slide.

"As of today, it's out with plain old J-u-l-i-e—I mean, really, who *doesn't* have that name? And it's in with J-u-l-é."

Julie looked incredulously back and forth between David, the screen, and RJ.

"You'll need to remember to pronounce it *Zhue-lay* when you talk to the press. *Zhue-lay* from EnChantay. Do you hear it? It has a singy quality."

"And finally," said Rachel, before Julie could answer, "we've saved the best for last. Alya, you are going to make the most amazing transformation. You know, David and I talked about you a lot and we said, you know, she's obviously really young, kind of unpredictable, a bit of a troublemaker, and we thought, *We love that,* and we want to push that further and give you this really cool, edgy, sharp look, like you're EnChantay's rad baby sister. And so what we came up with is—"

Whoa, hang on! What? Unpredictable? Troublemaker? Nuh-unh! How about "dependable" and "mature beyond her years"? That's what I was known for at home. That's what was written on my Rosewood report cards.

Rachel paused to throw the next sketch up. My jaw dropped.

"Yeah!" she said, pleased. "I knew that would get a reaction! So what we have here is—"

I didn't even hear her explanation—I was too shocked. Forget the glamour and glitz of big hair and freakish tuxedos. My costume was mostly construction boots.

"And then these little shorts . . ." Rachel's voice drifted back in over the loud screaming sound in my brain. "Loads of abs, like a fourteen-pack of abs, like there's eight bonus cans in there, but they're under this construction vest. And we're going to rub grease into everything, like *Who knows where she's been or what she's been doing?* You're down and dirty, gritty, not afraid to get a little grime under your nails," said Rachel. "But hot. So hot."

"Like we're ignoring sex so hard, it's all we can think about," said David.

"Oh, that is *so* you," said Ange. The now-familiar clamping feeling started to rise in my chest.

"For makeup," Rachel continued, "we're going to keep everything really light and fresh, but then we're going to make you look kind of sweaty and hot, again, like you could have been out running a marathon or boxing or rappelling down something—we don't really know. That's the whole beauty and mystery of your character.

"And I know you've got all these lovely braids, but we're going to have to pile them up under this trucker hat to preserve the illusion. And we'll top it all off with this rhinestone anarchy logo for that 'anything can happen' vibe."

Ange stifled a laugh.

I looked to RJ for some kind of reaction, but he was smiling at the screen, arms crossed over his chest. I ground my teeth together and stretched my lips so it looked like I was smiling. *Do not complain,* I told myself. *Whatever you do, do not complain. It will only make it worse.*

"Are there any questions?" asked RJ.

My hand shot up.

"Yes, Alya," he said, as if he was already growing very tired of me.

"This is all totally awesome and everything, like you said." I paused to smile like I really, really meant it. "But it seems like this isn't going to go with Raquo's choreography."

"No," said RJ, winking at Angelique. "It won't."

That's when he dropped the bomb: Raquo was fired.

"Mimi here is going to be your new dance captain," RJ said, and the fit woman at the end of the table waved shyly and smiled a frosted pink smile from beneath her dirty blonde bangs.

I gasped.

"The three of us are pretty much a team," said Rachel, gesturing to Mimi and David.

"But—" said Julie.

RJ waved her off. "Raquo hit his peak last year. He's old news. EnChantay is all about the *new* hotness. Mimi is *next year's* big choreographer, and we've got her *right now.* We're gonna break her, and every time someone hears the name Mimi Marcoux, they'll think EnChantay."

My hands started to shake, and my heart started to pound. These weren't little surface details. This was *everything.* Raquo was what got me excited to work with EnChantay in the first place. The choreography was *why* I'd put up with so much for so long—

"Is there a problem?" RJ asked. He sounded like he was very far away and talking in slow motion. The studio started to feel too small, like the walls were shrinking and the ceiling was getting closer.

"Are you okay, Alya?" Julie asked, leaning forward in her seat, into my space.

I pushed her away and stood up against the dizziness and the pressure building in my head.

"I need a glass of water," I whispered, and ran to the change room.

"Does she have a drug problem?" I heard David ask as the door swung shut behind me.

"That would be kind of hot," Rachel whispered, not quietly enough.

"And step touch, step touch, step touch, turn, and smile!" Mimi squeaked as she destroyed Raquo's choreography. "Oh my goodness, you're all so good! And shoulders, and shoulders, and shoulders, shake it!"

She had abandoned the vampire story and stripped the routine of its complexity, and with it, all of its sense.

"Now freeze and clench your tummies, so we can see your abs! And shimmy, shimmy!"

Raquo's ideas might have been a little out there, but at least he had ideas.

Ange put up her hand. "Mimi, can I bend over and arch my back instead of squatting and opening my knees?"

"Sure," said Mimi. "We'll change it. Julé, you do the squat thing instead, okay? And, Alya, you're still too smooth. I need you to rough it up, make it less feminine."

"That shouldn't be a problem for *her,*" Ange said under her breath. I looked her straight in the eye and challenged her to say it to my face. She looked away again.

"Chest-pop, chest-pop, grab your crotch, flip off the camera. Can I see you do that three more times?"

I did as she asked, and each time, I hated it a little more than the time before. It didn't make sense to act angry and "gritty"—whatever that meant—when there was nothing remotely gritty about the music.

"Alya, no," said Mimi. "No, no, no."

It shouldn't have bothered me so much. I was used to playing different roles for different pieces. But this wasn't supposed to be some character; this was supposed to be *me.*

RJ took over our final vocal rehearsal from Julé that week.

"All right, ladies," he said, "this is our last chance to practise before we go into the booth, so I want us all to really concentrate and put everything we have into making 'Steppin' Out' absolutely perfect."

"Hell, yeah!" said Ange, far too enthusiastically. Julé smiled tightly and cued up the beat. The all-too-familiar sound of our one track burst over the speakers. Ange began a voiceover I hadn't heard before:

Girl, listen I, uh . . . gotta tell you something—as your friend.
But, uh . . . you ain't gonna like this.

And I couldn't help feeling that she was speaking directly to me. In fact, all of the song's lyrics seemed to take on a different meaning. I could swear she looked right through me when she sang, *"But I got bad news, girl—you better think twice."*

"Hey yo! Whoa, whoa, whoa, whoa! Don't go getting nasty . . ." I sang halfheartedly, my emotions catching in my throat.

"Wait! Stop, stop, stop," said RJ, cutting the music. "Alya, I'm not hearing the passion when you sing *'let's keep it classy.'* Can you do it again, but with more passion?"

"Uh, sure," I said, trying to set aside my feelings and pull myself together. *It's just a song,* I told myself. *Use your feelings productively.*

"I know it hurts real bad," I sang, trying to underline *hurts,* then, *"but let's keep it classy,"* trying to get *classy* out heartfelt but delicate.

"No!" said RJ, abruptly. "Louder, harder. And I'm not feeling your pronunciation. *Clas-sy* just sounds too . . . classy. You're the gritty one—the thug. I need you to rough it up, make me feel the street. Try it this way: *class-eh.*"

"Classeh?"

"Yeah, exactly. Say the whole line."

"I know it hurts real bad, but let's keep it classeh?"

"You're still over-pronouncing. I don't want to hear every syllable. Make it street."

"Ah no it urts rill bad, bu les kip it class-heh?" I sang sarcastically.

"Yes!" he yelled. "Exactly!"

I looked over at Julé. She threw up her hands.

"See? That's what she does, 'cause she can't face the truth," Ange's voice accused.

"It's you I can't trust," Julé echoed over and over again.

"Whatcha, watcha gonna do?" demanded the trailing voiceover.

I didn't know what I was going to do, but I was pretty sure a group hug wasn't going to be the answer.

I didn't even recognize myself anymore. What had happened to the Alya who was always ahead? The one everyone said had so much potential? That Alya would never have followed Ange into that club and swallowed all those shots like she was Alice in Wonderland. Eat me. Drink me. Kiss me. If Angelique had been a guy, the old Alya would have told her, *Bite me.*

Twenty-three

When I saw Madi that weekend, it was really strange. I'd managed to avoid her the whole weekend before. I'd hidden in my room, sleeping all day, pretending I didn't feel well, which I guess was actually true on some level. I'd even skipped a Hydra Force practice. I knew I couldn't hide forever, but I had to hide at *least* until the bruise was gone. Makeup wasn't going to fool Madi, and neither would the "rehearsal accident" explanation I'd given my parents.

I might have tried to avoid her for a second weekend in a row, but she was too tenacious. She knew something was up. I knew she knew that something was up. I didn't know if she knew that I knew that she knew, but when she came over before practice on Saturday morning, she was fidgety, her smile hesitant. She fiddled with the zipper on her sweatshirt, dropping it only to hug me hello.

"What is going on with you? I feel like I haven't seen you in forever," she said, flinging herself across my bed, re-enacting normal.

I wondered, Did she already know exactly what was up? She was the one, after all, who had come up with the girl-crush theory. Was she just waiting for me to admit it?

"I know, almost two weeks. Crazy," I said, faking casual. Just because I had admitted it to myself didn't mean I was ready to deal with anyone else knowing—to have it picked apart and judged, and to have to defend myself, or even to have it celebrated, if that was the way it was going to go. It was mine, and only mine, to own.

"Soo . . ." she said in a leading tone, "what's new with EnChantay?" That was it. She knew. She definitely knew. Every muscle in my back tightened involuntarily.

"Not much," I said. It was, without a doubt, both the biggest and the shortest lie I had ever told her, and it hung in the room between us, not furthering the conversation, swelling with the bloat of every big thing I wasn't ready to tell her. I wished there could be a way to share just the safe parts: *I went to this crazy club. I met Bershawn.* But in my mind, all of that was bound up in everything bigger and more important. I knew I wouldn't be able to separate the strands once I started talking. So I kept my mouth shut.

"Really?" she said. Her expression was almost hurt. "Aren't you going into the studio soon? Hasn't RJ said anything weird? Is Angelique still hating on you?"

"We met the stylists this week," I offered.

"Cool!" she said, with renewed enthusiasm.

"Actually, it wasn't great," I told her. "The other girls have these glammed-out costumes, but me, I'm like this grungy person."

"Oh," she said. "That . . . sucks, I guess." She swallowed. "Um—"

"What?" I said.

"Are you sure there's nothing else going on? You seem kind of . . . sad, or weird, or something."

"I'm just tired," I snipped. "It was a long week—a long, *boring* week," I emphasized.

She looked at me as if she didn't quite buy it. "You've been 'tired' for, like, three weeks now."

I felt cornered. I laughed spitefully. "Yeah, 'cause, like

I've been trying to tell you, it's really freaking tiring. More than the Hydra Force, more than school."

"Okay, okay. Don't get mad," she said.

"Sorry," I said. "I'm just— What's new with you?"

"Um . . ." she said, "I got my full licence last week. I can drive on the highway now."

It was the kind of news that normally would have set us jumping around the room screaming and planning road trips. It was the kind of thing I normally would have known about already.

"That's great," I said. "I didn't even know you had taken the test."

"Oh yeah. Well, I was going to tell you but . . ."

But I had been avoiding her calls, letting my phone run dead, and not calling her myself when I had the chance. Fair enough.

"How are things with Trevor?" I asked.

"Good . . ." she said. "Good."

"Just good?" I prodded, finding a little of our old dynamic and latching onto it.

"Actually," she said, "I saw him last weekend at a show, and he asked me to come visit him again."

"Awesome!" I said. "When?

"Next week. He has Wednesday to Friday off. Then he's on the road again."

"Oh—" I said.

"What?" she said.

"Nothing. Just . . . we're recording next week, so if you want to hang out with me while you're there, I probably can't. I mean, I'm probably not allowed. Because of the schedule."

"Oh," she said. "Well, I'll be with Trevor anyway."

"If I have any free time at all, I'll spend it with you, if you want," I said quickly.

"Yeah. If I have time for a coffee or something, I'll let you know."

"Where are you going to stay?"

"At Trevor's."

That shocked me a little. "Really?" I asked. "Isn't it a bit soon? I mean—"

"Alya!" she squeaked, throwing one of my own stuffed bears at me. "His mom has a guest room."

"He lives with his *mom?*" I asked, picturing Ange's apartment. They were the same age . . .

She took a long pause. "Seriously, Al, why are you being like this? Are you mad at me?"

"No," I said. "It's just . . . I don't know. Don't you think things are moving kind of fast with him?"

She laughed. "If three dates in three months is fast, then yeah, I guess so. What's the matter? You don't want me in Montreal or something?"

"Of course not," I said.

"Okay, well, maybe we can drive home together on Friday? I'm taking the car. Because I can do that now." She grinned.

"You're allowed?" I asked.

"No."

I laughed.

"So are you in or what?"

I was a little scared at the prospect of spending six hours alone in a car with her at that point—that was a lot of time to not talk about something—but I didn't see any alternative. I couldn't keep pushing her away without giving her a reason.

"Okay, I'm in."

"Yay, half-road trip!" she said, sticking her hand up.

"Yay," I echoed tepidly, sealing it with our trademark high-five.

We started laying down the vocal track for "Girl Fight" at 9:00 a.m. on Monday, and we were still at it at 5:00 p.m. on Tuesday. It wasn't so much that things were going badly as it was that RJ wanted a billion takes of everything, especially from Angelique and Julé. At one point, he was even getting Julé to sing Angelique's vocals.

"Extra backup vocals," he explained, and then turned back to the mixing board.

Wednesday, we started shooting "real world" scenes for the video at Lucie Laittue, where I'd first had lunch with Angelique and Julie so many weeks before. The difference this time was that they both had to act like my friends, if only on camera.

"Okay, people," said the director. "So the concept is that you're best friends, and you're having an intervention because Julé's man here has been 'steppin' out' on her, and enough is enough, she needs to know. So you're chic, you're sexy, but most of all, you're concerned. This is a tear-jerker. I want to feel it."

He was partly right: Angelique and Julé were chic in designer jeans with heels, Angelique in a skin-tight tank, Julé drowning in a layered chiffon blouse that made her look like the clear loser between the two of them. I was wearing overalls over a sports bra, with weightlifting gloves. To brunch, apparently.

They had totally shut the place down to customers, blacked out the windows, and then flooded them with TV lights to simulate some kind of way-too-perky, blinding daylight. I felt for the Julé of the song. I knew from experience that a beautiful morning didn't help bad news go down any easier.

There was a coffee on the table in front of me, but I wasn't allowed to drink it. Food also, and we weren't allowed to touch it.

We had to sing along with the track we'd laid down in the studio the day before, but it didn't really matter what we sounded like, because they weren't going to use the audio. We just had to really look like we were singing. Between my scarce lines, I tried my best to act out "concerned badass baby sister friend," looking back and forth from one to the other, occasionally gesturing with a destination-less forkful of waffle. Then there were other scenes where we didn't sing at all but had to improvise, and I mimed out extreme concern, leaping out of my seat to keep them separated enough that Julé couldn't reach Angelique's hair to pull on it.

We had to stop for makeup touchups and I-don't-know-what delays every five minutes, so just this half of our two-minute song took all day to shoot. A few times it was my fault we had to do things twice.

"Alya, don't sit up too straight. It's not street."

Well, of course not. *I* wasn't street.

"Alya, pinkie down when you pick up that coffee to not drink it. You know what? Why don't you use both hands?"

I felt kind of dumb after a while, just watching Angelique and Julé like they were a tennis match, so I adopted an alternative pose, slouching down in the corner, chewing on a toothpick.

"Perfect!" David yelled. "Exactly!"

Madi arrived in town that night. She sent me a text to

let me know, but didn't suggest getting together or anything. I was relieved.

When I stepped into the studio the next morning, my jaw dropped.

It was incredible. The calm grey space where we'd been rehearsing for months had been utterly transformed into a shiny, slick black box. The windows had been blacked out, and from the floor to the ceiling there wasn't a single surface that didn't gleam and bounce back the bright white-and-pink light that projected from lamps hung from the ceiling and embedded in the floor.

In the middle of the space was an even shinier, slightly raised white box with gleaming chrome sides, blindingly lit from beneath.

Strands of what I can only describe as fishing line strung with shards of broken mirror rained down from the ceiling, spraying pinpoints of light around the room.

"You like it?" RJ asked, grinning, arms folded across his chest. I gaped.

A production assistant crossed the room at a run. "Ms. Merchant, we need you in wardrobe."

A wardrobe area had been set up behind some velvet curtains, near the original change room. Angelique and Julé were already there, each being fussed over by a different dresser.

I tried not to notice how amazing Angelique looked—all toned, bronze skin glittering with powder, high cheekbones, sharp lips, killer eyes. Her costume, which had appeared ridiculous on paper, looked stunning on her, as if it had improved itself on contact with her skin.

I turned quickly to Julé, who was looking considerably less comfortable in her sequined tuxedo pants with the slits up to her waist. If she stood perfectly still, she could almost make them hang straight, so she was rooted to one spot, muscles tensed, jaw locked, the tendons in her neck straining under the effort as a dresser fussed to pin her top hat to her head at a jaunty angle.

"Looking good," I lied.

"It's kind of drafty," she said.

"It looks totally natural on you," I said, to be nice. She relaxed and the pants flared, baring her fishnet-clad legs.

I grabbed my costume off the rack. Jeans. Blah. Tank top. Blah. Hat, blah. Work boots, blah. The makeup artist put away her brushes and glitter, locked all the pretty golds and pinks up in her makeup case, and then turned to me with a palette of "darks and shadows."

"All right," she said, "let's get you done." I closed my eyes and submitted to the depressing transformation.

It's all for the music, I told myself.

I joined Angelique and Julé in the centre of the lit-up white cube. Around us, technicians in black rushed to tape down cable. Lights were adjusted, makeup was retouched, cameras were wheeled into position.

"Hey, gang," said choreographer Mimi, lazily striding towards us in her stretch jeans and leg warmers. "Just a couple of notes from David and RJ before we get going today. We're going to change around your positions in the choreo a little. Angelique, from now on, you're going to stand at the front, and Alya and Julé will stand behind you. That way, on camera you'll all appear to be more or less the same height, and I think people won't notice Julé's age so much."

Julé smiled through clenched teeth.

"Is that okay, Angie, hon? I don't want you to feel overexposed."

"Yeah, sure, I guess," she said coyly, as if she wasn't lapping up the attention.

I held back a laugh and scowled a little harder.

"Alya, excellent attitude," said Mimi. "Keep that face all day if you can. That's perfect."

I frowned a little harder.

"Brilliant!" said Mimi.

Julé shrank farther to the back.

"Exactly, Julé," said Mimi. "Memorize that mark."

Our music played and the cameras rolled. Angelique faked, rushed, stumbled, and flailed her way through the choreography, using her hair and her breasts as decoys. It was as though the easier the steps had become, the less she had practised, so she was still just as behind as she had been with Raquo. It was so frustrating to watch that it was all I could do to keep myself from grabbing her by the waist and shoving her to where she was supposed to be on each count.

If I'd had more to do, I might not have cared, but my own part had been trimmed back so far I was practically standing still—a backdrop for her failure.

"Shoulder, shoulder, fist," Mimi yelled at me, as if I was going to forget. "Angrier, Alya. Angrier!"

I played a game in my head where every time I took a step, I pictured a hungry tiger or charging rhinoceros.

"Good, Alya. Let's see that animal instinct."

I pinched my mouth closed like an anteater and threw up my arms like a gorilla. I was an entire zoo of animal instinct.

I left the studio that day telling myself that I shouldn't get upset—that I couldn't see what the director was seeing, that I should reserve judgment for the final product, that it was normal to have to do things you didn't like when you were as new as I was, that I was acting, acting, acting, and no one would really believe that was me out there.

When I got back to Dee's, I went for a run to blow off some steam, then had a really long, very hot shower (to inhale some new steam, ha).

Then my phone rang: Madi.

"How was day two of the shoot?" she asked.

"Brutal," I said.

"You must be exhausted," she said.

"Yeah."

"Do you want to come meet us for ice cream or something? We're in the neighbourhood."

"You are? Where?"

"Uh, Berri and—"

"I'm not near Berri."

"You're not? I thought you said the dorm—"

"I'm not staying in the dorm anymore, remember?"

"Um, no," she said. "You didn't tell me."

A sinking feeling set in as I realized she was right. "I'm staying with Dee now. On the other side of town."

She was quiet for longer than it's comfortable for someone to be quiet on a phone. Then she asked simply, "Why?"

"It's homier here."

"That's it? There's *no* other reason?"

"No."

"Are you sure?"

"Yeah."

"Are you absolutely sure you're okay?"

"Yeah."

"Why didn't you say anything before?"

"I keep telling you, I'm tired. Maybe someday when you have a real job, you'll understand," I snapped.

"I should go," she said. "Trevor is waiting. I'll call you tomorrow about driving home."

"Okay," I said. "Have a good time with Trevor."

The next morning, I was met at the studio by RJ, David, Rachel, and Mimi. There was no one else there but a couple of guys to run the cameras and lights. There was no sign of Angelique or Julé or any of the production assistants who had been running around the day before, making "the magic" happen. The studio had a chilled, unsettled air—it was too quiet and too still. The transformation that had looked so shiny and exciting the day before gave off an almost sinister vibe in the quiet.

"What's going on?" I asked RJ.

"We only need you today. Angie and Julé have the day off."

"Oh, okay," I said.

Rachel beckoned me over to the wardrobe area, where she handed me a costume that I could have sworn was an exact replica of Angelique's.

"We need you to put this on," she said.

"But . . . why?" I asked.

"Just do it, Alya," RJ called over the curtain.

"David might cut a version with everyone in the same costumes, so they want to get extra footage in the can," whispered Rachel.

"But what about—?"

"Enough questions, Alya," RJ barked. "Put on the costume *now*. We don't have time for this."

My phone rang in my bag. I didn't dare answer it.

With Rachel watching me, blocking the only exit, arms crossed over her chest, I stripped down to my underwear. She helped me ease into the fishnets, the push-up bra, the skirt, the boots, and the sequined jacket. I was surprised to find how cramped the boots were, how scratchy the jacket. The bra jabbed me in the ribs, and the skirt was so tight it was hard to walk.

I stared at myself in the change room mirror. Had I really been jealous of this costume? I felt ridiculous. Although there was scratchy, pinchy costume exploding all over the place, all that really stood out were my abs, thighs, and cleavage. Where tiny Ange glowed and scintillated and demanded attention, gigantic Alzilla me clomped around, glittering too hard, like a second-rate drag queen.

Rachel stepped forward and assaulted me with the wig and headpiece, which made me look like I had fifty golden, starry tentacles. It squeezed my head, pulling my eyebrows up into a non-negotiable expression of surprise.

"Don't forget your gloves," she said, handing them to me. "They're ready for you. Follow me."

Pulling on the gloves, which were latex and fought me every dainty, teetering step of the way, I followed her as best I could, feeling like I might fall and crush Tokyo in the slightest breeze.

"She's really a lot taller, isn't she?" Mimi said to RJ as I took my position towards the back of the white cube.

"Sweetie, can you come take your mark up here?" she said, pointing to where Angelique usually stood.

"But—"

"Alya," said RJ. "No arguing."

"Okay," said Mimi, "so we're just going to shoot a few key sequences and then you can go, okay, honey?"

Sure, darling, I almost responded, but opted instead for a nod.

The lights came on again and the music burst over the stereo. It took me a few tries to work out how to do the choreography right in heels.

"Sweetheart, sugar," said Mimi, "you can leave the shoulders and everything out of it just this time."

I nodded and ran it again, surprised to discover how hard it was to drop the "attitude" now that I'd learned it.

As I watched Mimi and RJ, their heads bowed together over a clipboard, covering their mouths so I couldn't see what they were whispering, a lump formed in my throat.

I knew it then: there wasn't going to be any cut with everyone in matching costumes. They were using me as Angelique's body double, for the feet, at least. The steps I had tried to help her learn I would dance for her now, just as Julie had sung the notes she couldn't reach. And someday, when it was over, I would still have dancing, and Julie would still have singing, and Angelique would have EnChantay.

Over the fifteen minutes I had for lunch, I checked my messages. Madi said if she didn't hear from me, she'd meet me at the train station at 5:30. Then I had to turn my ringer off, under RJ's threat of confiscating my phone. I didn't even hear the next three calls I missed. I moved through the rest of the day like a zombie drone, doing what I was told, thinking only of not thinking about it. I was finally allowed to go at 5:30, half an hour late. I grabbed my things and rushed down the stairs, and up and over the ten blocks to the train station.

Twenty-four

Madi was waiting, just as she had promised. I knocked on the window and she unlocked the door for me. I got in. She didn't look at me.

"Alya! I'm amazed you showed up."

"I'm so sorry—" I started.

"Not as sorry as I am," she said, angrily putting the car in gear. "This whole trip was a big mistake."

"Why? What happened with Trevor?" I asked.

"Just that we broke up," she said quietly, rushing a yellow light to turn onto the highway.

"What?" I said as the car was swallowed by a tunnel.

"Last night when we were out, not having ice cream with you, he ran into his ex-girlfriend."

"So?"

"She was back from some trip. India or Indonesia. I don't know. It was loud where we were. Anyway, he invited her to sit with us, and I guess that's when he realized he still liked her, because for the rest of the night it was like I wasn't even there. On our way back to his place, he was all Anne-Marie this, Anne-Marie that."

"Madi, that's awful!" I said. "I had no idea—"

"Of course you didn't. You don't answer when I call anymore."

"I tried—"

"Whatever. When we talk lately, you sound bored. Or distracted. Or busy. Or like you just don't care."

"I care, Madi! I'm your best friend."

"No. We used to be best friends. Now you're more like some girl I used to know, who used to know me. You avoid me. You don't tell me anything." She started to cry. The car swerved disconcertingly towards the wall of the tunnel each time she swiped at her eyes with her sleeve. "This sucks. I never thought I'd lose two people in the same weekend."

"It's not like that," I said. "You haven't lost me. I'm not avoiding you." *Anymore,* I completed in my head.

"Well, what is it then? What happened? Why can't you talk to me anymore? What did I do?"

"You didn't do anything. It's not you."

"Then what is it?"

"I—"

I tried to think up an answer she'd believe, but I was out of lies. As the car left the tunnel and we emerged into the dim evening light, I realized that I was running out of options.

1) I could pretend I didn't need her, not tell her, and find a whole new set of friends.

2) I could keep inventing more and more complicated reasons not to tell her, and resign myself to living in secret forever, like Bershawn or, worse, Angelique.

As far as I could tell, both options meant basically the same thing: I could let go of the truth or actually become the lie.

"What?" she yelled. "What is it you have to think over? Why can't you just tell me?"

"I like girls," I finally said.

"So?" she said, anticlimactically, and I realized I hadn't been clear enough.

The road curved westward, and the setting sun suddenly threatened to bore a hole in my retinas. I felt my cheeks heat up as I slid farther down into my seat. *I've changed my mind!* I wanted to yell. *I'm not ready for this! Undo! Undo!*

But I knew by the way she was glancing over at me furiously, keeping just one squinting eye on the road, that it was now or never.

"No, Madi," I corrected. "I *like* girls. I liked Angelique like you liked Trevor."

Her eyes widened.

"You mean you *like* her like her?"

"Yes. Well, no. Yes."

"But you said you didn't have a crush!"

I shrug-squirmed, hoping the worst was over. She opened her mouth as if to argue, then closed it, opened it, closed it, opened it, frowned, and finally drove in silence for something like ten kilometres. I sat perfectly still and watched the reflector strips on the road start to glow under the headlights as blue evening sky turn into black night.

"Madi?" I finally said. "Please say something."

"Are you sure?" she asked. "What if it's just stress?"

That totally caught me off guard. "Stress?" I repeated. "Like I'm so *busy* I *forgot* to be into guys? Or like being into girls is a disorder?"

She bit her lip. "Well, I mean, how would you know you don't want to be with guys when you've never dated one seriously?"

I glared at her. "How do you know you don't like girls when you've never dated one seriously?"

She ignored my question. "But what if you just haven't met the right guy? Or what if you're bi?"

"Madi, I'm not bi. I like girls. I don't want to meet any more guys."

"You say that now, but it could just be a phase."

"Okay," I told her. "Forget I brought it up. Forget I said anything. I should have known you'd be like this."

"Be like what? I just don't want you to jump to conclusions. I mean, I wasn't into Trevor at first, but you convinced me to give him a chance. Maybe this is like that."

"I said forget it."

"Al—"

"No, drop it. Forget I said anything. I didn't tell you for you to talk down to me."

"I'm not—"

I turned my back to her, bunched my sweater up, and used it as a pillow, leaning my head against the window.

"Al—"

I didn't react. I pretended I was sleeping. And before long, I was.

When I woke up, I almost couldn't see out of the car, it was raining so hard. Every window was blurry grey. Only the taillights of other cars were visible, crawling by in the rain.

"Where are we?" I asked.

"I don't know," she said.

"Are we late?"

"I'd assume so. We've been going only thirty clicks for the last hour and a half."

"But, Madi, I'm not even supposed to be in this car with you. You know how my parents are about 'new drivers.' If we don't beat Devin to the train station—"

"Then he'll have to cover for you. Call him if you're worried."

I reluctantly fished my phone out of my bag and stared at it for a while before deciding to dial. It might not have been a big deal for normal people, but my parents were not normal. If I told Devin where I was, he was going to have me doing favours for him until I was eighty, whether or not we were actually late. But I couldn't have my family thinking I'd gone missing. I called.

"Network connection error," said a robotic voice on the other end of the phone.

"I can't get through!" I told Madi.

"Try mine," she said.

I dialled. Same problem.

Outside, the wind picked up and the car shook.

"If it gets any worse, I'm going to have to pull over."

"But if we don't make it in time, I'm going to be so dead. We're going to be so dead. Did you even tell your mom you were taking the car?"

"No." She huffed. "But if I drive any faster, we'll be even deader."

I sat back again and saw that it was hopeless. We were going to be late. I was going to be dead. I would be dead with no crush and no best friend. My parents would be too mad to throw me a proper funeral. I would be remembered for chewing a toothpick and grabbing my crotch. Angelique would keep my feet forever.

I shook out my sweater and curled up under it like a blanket.

"Do you want me to turn on the radio?" I asked Madi.

She sighed. "Okay, but not too loud."

"Are you thirsty? I've got a juice box in my bag."

"No, I'm fine."

Brow furrowed in concentration, Madi drove on

through the night. We didn't speak. I lost track of time. I kept trying to call Devin, but I never got through.

By the time the storm let up, we were so late the trains had already stopped running, and then we were mired in Toronto traffic. When the exit to Rivercrest came up—almost twenty minutes before the exit for Guildwood station—Madi took it.

"Not much point now in pretending you're on a train."

I agreed silently.

Our parents were waiting for us when Madi's car finally turned into my driveway. They came pouring out of my front door in a thick, angry parental mob and yanked us from our seats. I was dragged inside and Madi was shoved into the back of the car and driven next door before our front door had even closed.

"*What,*" my mother demanded, "is the meaning of this?"

But I knew better than to speak before knowing what they knew.

"Not even a phone call to let us know where you were! Your brother went all the way to the station in this storm. We were five minutes from calling the police!"

"I tried. The network was down."

"It wouldn't have mattered if you had just got on that train like you were supposed to," said my father. "Instead, you're joyriding all over the place with Madison. Even RJ didn't know where you were. Do you know how dangerous that is? Taking off without letting anyone know where you're going to be? If you're supposed to be on a train, we expect you to be on a train, not in a car with a new driver—"

"A *stolen* car I might add! No one at Madison's even

knew the car was missing! Honestly, I don't know what's come over the pair of you."

"And *then* we hear from RJ how you've been partying it up in Montreal"

"That's what he told you?"

"Drinking!"

"Showing up over two hours late!"

"Getting this other girl, Angelique, in trouble."

"Is *that* what RJ told you?"

"This is who you are now? This is what you do with your freedom?"

"That's not what happened," I said. "Not like that."

The vein in my dad's forehead bulged purple.

"Why should we believe a word you say? Go to bed, before we say something we regret."

I slept the sleep of the so-dead. When I finally woke up, it felt like waking up for the first time ever.

I wiggled my toes and unglued my eyes. Slowly, everything un-stiffened. I had lived. I was alive.

My phone dinged. A text message.

MadMadi: "RU OK?"

I rolled over on my side and awkwardly thumbed back in the dark:

"I'm OK. RU OK?"

MadMadi: "Is this OK? Im txtng bcuz I'm grounded from talking to u."

"Oh no!"

MadMadi: "I'm OK tho. It's OK."

"OK."

MadMadi: "I'm SO SORRY 4 giving u a hard time ystrdy. I was an a-hole. I luv u no matter who u like."

Tears started to well up in my still sleep-heavy eyes.

"No, I'm sorry," I texted back. "I jerked u around all month. I'm the a-hole."

MadMadi: "Is that possible? Can we both be a-holes?"

"I'm sorry about Trevor."

MadMadi: "me too."

"If there's anything I can do let me know."

MadMadi: "next time, set me up with someone LOCAL."

"Good idea."

MadMadi: "Thanks 4 telling about Ange. I want you to be able to tell me things. Even if I am uncomfortable."

"Are you?"

MadMadi: "A little? I feel kinda stupid, like it was obvious."

"How could you know if I didn't?"

MadMadi: "that's what friends r for. I shoulda noticed. OMIGOD!"

"What?"

MadMadi: "I know this grrl u should totally call!"

"Madi! No!"

MadMadi: "2 comfy 2 soon?"

MadMadi: "<<HUG>> If u get another crush will u tell me?"

"Will u stop me if she's anything like Ange?"

MadMadi: "Deal. Promise u won't disappear again."

"Deal. If I ever get some grls name tattooed on my body it'll be yours and not some grls."

MadMadi: "I will remind u of this 18r."

"BFF?"

MadMadi: "BBBBBBBBFF."

My parents and I had a conference call with RJ the next morning. On the agenda:

1. How bad I'd screwed up.
2. Whose fault it was I'd screwed up.
3. How I was going to be disciplined.

RJ opened the conversation by telling them how sullen and uncooperative I'd been for the last few weeks.

"Can I say something?" I said.

"Don't interrupt," they said.

"I quit," I interrupted.

My parents exchanged a confused look. This wasn't in the plan. My dad flipped through his notes. Nope. Nothing in the notes.

I was so done easing into touchy subjects. I think you could spend a whole life just trying to ease from one touchy thing to the next.

"I'm sorry, *what?*" said RJ, like he hadn't even considered the possibility. As if all those EnChantay girls before me—the ones who didn't "work out"—had been straight up fired. "You can't just quit!" he said, his voice rising into his nose like it did when he was stressed.

"Okay, then I'm fired."

"Is this about money?"

"No."

My father leaned forward and cleared his throat uncomfortably.

"Is it because you don't have enough lines?" asked RJ.

"No."

"Everyone can't be the star, you know. I told you that," he said.

"I think what Alya's trying to say—" my mother started.

But I already knew what I was trying to say. I loved performing, but I also loved life—real life—my family, my friends, the Hydra Force, the stinky b-boy van, all the summer reading I hadn't done for Rosewood, my own style, my own strengths. On its own, each of those things sounded like a tiny detail, but I realized that what it all added up to was that I wasn't like Angelique, who only wanted to be famous, or Julie, who only wanted to make music, or RJ, who only wanted to be "hot." I didn't want only one thing. I wanted all of those things, and a life, and my own ideas. And if wanting all of them meant I could only have a tiny piece of each one, or I could only have them one at a time, or I could only have them later, I could wait. It wasn't business to me. It was everything.

"You're making a terrible mistake," said RJ. "Do you know how many girls dream about this stuff? *Anyone* can be a student. *Anyone* can be some anonymous b-girl in some shitty crew. It takes someone special to be in EnChantay, and everyone is going to know that."

I didn't bother arguing. Instead, I said, "Maybe my spot would be better occupied by someone who can really appreciate it."

At that, my mother seemed to see me with fresh eyes. My dad put his pen down and leaned back in his chair.

"Is this because you're afraid you can't do it?" RJ asked.

"No," I said. I had learned to sing. That was me who had put in all those hours of training. I loved the spotlight. And *because* I loved the spotlight, I didn't want it to shine on garbage. Having finally realized I *could* do it, I couldn't just hand myself over like a smooth lump of putty to be pounded and prodded and forced into any shape and sold however they wanted—not when I hadn't even tried to succeed as myself yet. Maybe it was true that you had to give up a big piece of yourself to make it. Maybe one day I'd agree with that. But I sure as hell wasn't about to *start out* working towards that!

"Do you have any idea the resources we've wasted on you?" shouted RJ. "You're all over the goddamn video!"

"Isn't it better that I leave now, before I'm all over the album, too?" I said as soothingly as I could.

"Your contract—" started RJ.

My dad cut him off. "Mr. Cormier, I think we'd better have our lawyers take it from here. I think my daughter has made it clear what she wants. There's no point in pressuring her."

"If you had better control over her, Wallace—" said RJ. "Then again," he muttered to himself, "the controversy could be kind of hot. I could launch the group *twice.*"

"Good day, Mr. Cormier."

"You'll never get another opportunity like this."

I smiled. I was okay with that.

I texted Madi when it was all over.

MadMadi: "OMG. I am so proud of U. Ur still a star to me."

MadMadi: "Did you tell ur mom ur gay?"

"Did u get ur invite to PFLAG yet?"

MadMadi: "So that's a no? Your dad?"

"I don't want him chasing me with rainbow pins."

MadMadi: "Devin?"

"I already know what he'd say."

MadMadi: "Just cuz ur a dyke don't mean ur not a butthead?"

"Hey!"

MadMadi: "He *would* say that."

"I just want it to be my thing for now. OK?"

MadMadi: "OK."

"Ur not allowed to tell them."

MadMadi: "I said OK!"

"Ur not allowed to hint either."

MadMadi: "I don't do that!"

"???????"

MadMadi: "OK, I *won't* do that."

The video single came out two months later. The Hydra Force threw me a release party. Since I still wasn't allowed in Madi's house, we gathered around GruvTV in Nadine's basement. There was milk and cookies, and her baby sister danced for us during the commercials. My parents came, too.

It was hard to watch. Half of the video was Angelique making out with some guy in slow motion—the guy who was supposed to be making out with the video version of Julé, while (in a perfect world) *I* was supposed to be making out with Ange.

The choreography had been cut way back. And when Angelique sang, Julé's voice came out of her mouth. When she danced, the camera closed in on my feet.

I should have hated her, but my first thought was that she was still beautiful. I still had to watch her. I still thought about her after. I was glad she was very far away.

After the video, there was an in-studio interview with Angelique, Julé, and some girl who was not me. Only Angelique spoke. Julé beamed and nodded like she agreed with everything Angelique said, even when Angelique explained how they'd been friends since kindergarten and described how Julé had inspired her to write "Girl Fight" after a late night heart-to-heart about a bad relationship. The girl who was not me said nothing. She just skulked in the back with her hands in the pockets of her baggy jeans, her eyes barely visible beneath the brim of her Canadiens hat.

Nadine's parents were shocked at the "skimpy costumes." My parents were outraged I didn't have more screen time. Madi and Nadine were angry that the song "perpetuated the sexist myth that women are catty."

I just smiled because it was over.

I saw Angelique only one more time after that. It was at the Hogtown Throwdown, the biggest b-boy battle of the year. I had returned to b-girling with a vengeance. I wasn't just a hip-hopper with skills any more—I was owning it. EnChantay's first show in Toronto was that night, and I hadn't even noticed the listing, I'd been so wrapped up in life. We had just found out the results of the semifinal (we won), when I heard her call out my name.

"Alya!"

I whipped around, sure I was imagining it, but there she stood, across the gym, a tiny haute-couture wand topped with a pompom of hair.

I waited for her to cross the gym to me.

"Did you just win that?" she asked. "That was . . . I could never do that."

I realized that was how she saw the world: in terms of things she couldn't do and people she couldn't beat. Anything she couldn't conquer or ignore, she had to destroy or disable.

She fiddled with the trim on her jacket, wobbling a little on the spiky heels of her boots.

"I'm really sorry for . . . what . . . happened," she said.

"Ancient history," I said. It was more than I'd ever expected from her.

"I promise I won't tell anyone," she said.

I smiled what might have been a slightly evil smile. "I don't care if you tell anyone," I said, and let her worry about that for a few seconds before finishing my thought. "But I won't either." Dee and Madi didn't count. They had my back.

Angelique and I stared at each other a moment longer. Despite the way I puffed out my chest and held up my chin, it was definitely still there—that terrible, gripping thing that had attracted me to her in the first place. But now I could also see the pimple her foundation couldn't quite cover up, the roots where her dye job was growing out, and more than anything, the panic behind her eyes.

"Well, good luck with . . . this," she said, gesturing as if she had to escape soon, before the unholy grass-rootsiness of it all rubbed off on her. "I have to go to sound check."

"Have a good show," I said. "Tell Julie I say hi."

"Okay," she said, and strode back across the gym on her clicking heels. A line of drooling b-boys fell after her like dominoes. She looked over her shoulder at me one last time. Our eyes met for one final second. Then she looked away sharply, and she was gone.

A sigh of relief left my body. I might not have known exactly where I was headed, but at least I wasn't afraid of wherever it would turn out to be, or who I might find when I got there.

Smiling to myself, I rejoined the Force in the circle at the centre of the gym.

That's when I noticed her watching me. At least I think she was—a tall, lean girl with pixie hair and a tiny rainbow pin on her camera strap. I smiled at her, and she smiled back, self-consciously.

Devin ran up behind me with Nadine and Madi and punched me in the shoulder.

"Yo, butthead, we're grabbing lunch. You coming?"

"I'll be there in a minute," I said.

Madi followed my gaze across the gym.

"Oh yeah!" she said, then covered her mouth like she'd given away a secret. But I didn't care.

As the Force ran off, I crossed the gym to where the camera girl was standing.

The redo starts now, I thought to myself, and held out my hand.

"Hi," I said. "I'm Alya."

Acknowledgements

Mille mercis to my indispensable friend-and-agent, Sarah Heller, my editor, Amy Black, and to Kristin Cochrane and everyone at Doubleday Canada.

Thanks to my friend-and-vocal coach, Amanda Mabro, for inspiration, education and loving my dog.

No thanks to that dog for eating 12 foil cupcake wrappers in one sitting.

Thanks to the friends-and-dancers who appeared with me in support of *Break On Through*: Eva "MaeHem" Nikitova, JoDee "Feisty" Allen, Andrea "Skribbs" Bellemare & Stephan "Bboy#2" Lavoix.

Thanks to *all* my friend-ands, for being awesome, interesting and motley.

Thanks to my family for still being willing to be related to me when I'm cranky.

Thanks to *their* friends for accepting my books as gifts on all festive occasions.

Thanks to the nice people at Via Rail for providing an affordable, sustainable transit option between Montreal and Toronto, even if I am as sick of "the corridor" as Alya is.

And finally, to mes amis, collègues et clients @Transcon, merci for votre support, flexibilité, et surtout for saying nice things about my baking.

All you people are lifelines.